GO SHE MUST!

Also by David Garnett

LADY INTO FOX
A MAN IN THE ZOO
THE SAILOR'S RETURN

GO SHE MUST!

*

DAVID GARNETT

LONDON

CHATTO & WINDUS

1927

TO
STEPHEN TOMLIN

Contents

GO SHE MUST!

Chapter 1

BIRDS IN THE SNOW

SNOW lay thick over everything on the morning of the second Monday in the year, and the Reverend Charles Dunnock, drawing back the curtains of his bedroom window, said to himself that if the great sycamore full of rooks' nests in the church-yard were to fall, or even if a steeple were to be built for the little church of Dry Coulter, such changes would not alter the landscape so much as this snowstorm had done. Buried under three inches of snow the country was recognizable, but wholly transformed, and he asked himself how it was that a uniform colouring should make a totally new world yet one which was composed of familiar objects in their accustomed places.

Indifferent to the cold, he gazed out of his bedroom window enchanted by the beauty of the scene, and then, as he caught a glimpse of the first horizontal beams of the sun falling on Nature's wedding-cake, he told himself that even the dullest witted of his dissenting parishioners would feel compelled to cry out: " This is like Heaven! I could fancy myself dead, and this Eternity! "

" Yes "—he reflected—" all men must feel it, for that conceit is helped out by the extraordinary stillness, the footfalls of man and bird and beast are muffled, and the world seems empty. Nobody is stirring, for there is nothing like a heavy fall of snow to keep people by their firesides. Only the postman and the milkman go their rounds " ; and while he was dressing he heard their sudden knocks at the back door, with no warning crunch of gravel, or sound of the gate slamming in the yard.

" Their fidelity," he said to himself, " is like that of the clocks striking the hours when there is death in the house "—for Mrs. Dunnock had died exactly a year before, and her death was always in his mind. His bedroom had been her bedroom, though only for a few months, for she had died soon after her husband had been presented with a living, and since her death he slept alone in the great bed where she had waited so often for him to come up from his study, and where he had always found her with her soft hair spread

2

like a bird's wing over the pillow, and in which she had died

" The clocks strike the hours in the moments of our greatest sorrow," he said to himself. " Nothing will keep them from the punctual discharge of their duty, and listening to them we are recalled to this life, we shoulder our burdens once more, we begin ticking again ourselves, ticking away our ordinary lives."

He went to the looking-glass hanging over *her* dressing-table and began to comb his beard, then, looking once more out of the window, watched two men pass by, leading a horse along the road to be roughed at the blacksmith's, a slow business, for one of the men had to throw down sacks every few yards for it to step on, wherever the blizzard had whirled away the snow and left a polished slide of ice.

At a few minutes before nine he sat down to the breakfast table and took the cup of tea that his daughter poured out for him; then, hearing a shout, both Anne and he turned to the window and caught sight of a red muffler flying in the wind, and a thrown snowball, but when the children had passed, running on their way to school, all was silence, for Mr. Dunnock had turned to read a circular which the postman had brought that morning.

"Evangelicals! Evangelicals!" he muttered angrily, for he was a ritualist; a last flicker of the Oxford Movement had filled his life with poetry. Then he pushed away the newspaper and taking some bread for the birds, he rose from the breakfast table and went to the front door.

The world outside was dazzling, and the snow lay piled up deep before the sill. Mr. Dunnock peered out, not daring to step in the snow in his carpet slippers. He listened: not a sound; he looked and marked the roofs which yesterday were but the edges of a row of tiles, to-day as thick as thatch—like Christmas cards. "And here's a robin," he said, "waiting for me to throw him some of the bread." He threw a piece which was lost in the snow. "A wedding-cake! How strange it is to reflect that Anne is older now than her mother when I married her! Yes, the world is become a wedding-cake. Something very strange has happened, and who knows what will be the end of it, for it has begun to snow again, and the rare flakes drift slowly to the ground like feathers from the angels' wings. Are they

4

moulting up there? Or has Satan got among them like a black cat which has climbed through the wire netting into the dove loft? "

Mr. Dunnock fetched a piece of cardboard from his study to serve as a table for the birds, and dropped it a few feet away onto the snow, then crumbling the bread in his fingers, he threw the birds their breakfast. Some of the crumbs fell on each side into the snow and were lost.

" Here they come," he said to himself, for bright eyes had been watching him from every tree and bush.

The birds fluttered nearer, eyeing the crumbs spread out for them, and then looking sideways at the tall, bearded man standing in the doorway. Their fear was speedily forgotten, for the clergyman made it his habit to feed them every morning, and soon the cardboard table was covered with sparrows, robins, blackbirds, and thrushes, all of them flashing their wings, bickering and scrambling for the finest crumbs like a flock of bantams. And having been successful, one would often fly off with a piece in his bill, which he wished to devour in solitude.

Anne Dunnock remained at the break-

fast table, for she had only just finished
the kipper on her plate. "The labourers
will not go to work in the fields on such
a day as this," she said to herself. "And
not a woman will venture out except me,
for women's boots are generally leaky,
and their skirts flap wet against their
calves. With a frost like this there should
be skating, but the snow will have spoilt
the ice, even if it were swept." She finished
a piece of toast and rose from the table
to clear away the breakfast. The loaf was
a pitiful object, only a shell of crust, with
all of the inside scooped out.

"Another loaf gone," she said to herself. "We always have stale crusts, yet I
am sure the birds would eat them as readily as they do the crumb, and crusts are
so nasty in bread-and-butter pudding."

Mr. Dunnock continued watching the
birds, and the draught from the open
front door made his daughter shiver.
"Birds! Birds! I should like to wear a
bird in my hat."

She was a tall girl, beautiful, with a
small pale face, and straw-coloured hair,
hair which would not stay up; wherever
she went she scattered hairpins. She was
still in mourning for her mother's death,

and her long black dress fitted her badly, hindering her impatient movements, and giving her the look of a converted savage dressed in a missionary's night-gown.

" Father is feeding the birds. He never forgets them, and here am I grudging them the crumb of the loaf. But house-keeping would have made Saint Francis uncharitable, though Saint Francis would not have said he wanted a bird for his hat."

The marmalade, the cruet, the silver toast rack, all were put away into the mahogany sideboard, the tablecloth was brushed, and holding the little wooden tray full of crumbs, she went out into the hall, where her father still stood at the open door, and then leaning over his shoulder she shook the crumbs out onto the snow, and, scared by her sudden gesture, the birds flew off.

" Oh, Anne, how stupid and inconsiderate you are! " exclaimed her father, angrily. " How little imagination you have. Don't you understand that when you wave anything suddenly like that you frighten them. There was such a fine missel-thrush too. He is not regular, and though the other birds will soon come back, he will be discouraged. It is most vexing." Now that Mr. Dunnock had lost his congregation (a far larger one than had ever attended a Communion service at Dry Coulter Church), he shut the door, shaking his head irritably, then he put his beard in his mouth, as if that were the best way to stifle his anger, and went into his study.

The book he took up fell from his hands before he had turned the second or third page, for he had not the intellect nor the determination to be a scholar. A beautiful word always set his mind chasing a beautiful picture; his thoughts clouded over with dreams, and he remained lost in meditation. When he came to himself it was to sink onto his knees in prayer, for he was a shy man, unable to express himself to men, and for that reason much given to communing with God.

For twenty years he had been a poor curate at a church in the shadow of Ely Cathedral, but he had not been popular: he was indifferent to the things which were important to his fellow clergy, and his mystical love of ritual had found no sympathisers, until at last the Bishop took pity on him, and gave him a small living in a district in the fens. His growing uncertainty of temper, combined with a sort of hopeless oddity, had begun to make him a nuisance, and some provision had to be made.

At Ely the Church is taken seriously: it is a great power, and on taking up his new position, Mr. Dunnock was shocked to find it completely disregarded, for the inhabitants of Dry Coulter are Nonconformists. Even with the few who belonged to the church, he was not a success. His sermons were incomprehensible, yet they might have passed unnoticed if he had not affected a cassock and a biretta, if he had not placed a crucifix on the Communion table and called a blessing on the houses of the sick before he entered them. As vicar Mr. Dunnock was a failure, and within less than a year he was regarded with far greater contempt than is usually extended to the clergy. Yet he was not a disappointed man, for he had never been ambitious of success, and had never imagined that he might be popular. He knew that it was too late in his life for him to make any great effort; he was disinclined to exert himself with his parishioners, and avoiding them as far as he could, he was not unhappy. He had grown lazy, too, and now that it was in his power, he neglected to hold the innumerable little services which as a curate he had longed to celebrate.

If his wife had lived he might perhaps have exerted himself, but he knew that Anne did not share his emotions, and soon the special days were passed over, and Mr. Dunnock remained sunk in melancholy. Sometimes his conscience pricked him; then he shut himself up in his room and remained for hours in prayer.

"Damn the missel-thrush!" thought his daughter. "But father is always irritable on Mondays; I have noticed it before. Life indeed would be intolerable if it were not for the house. I have everything to make me unhappy, but I love this house. Dear old Noah's ark."

She went upstairs, where Maggie was waiting for her to help in making the beds. Maggie Pattle was a girl of seventeen, who lived out with her mother, and let herself into the vicarage early every morning, for she was the only servant and came in by the day. Shorter than Anne, she was fully twice as broad, a well-nourished girl, who would eat a pound of sausages or of bacon at a sitting, washing it down with vinegar, and her red cheeks shone with health.

Anne often thought that if only Maggie had come from another village she would have made an excellent servant; all her sluttish ways came from her mother's being just round the corner; she had only to slip down the vicarage garden, and through a hole in the hedge to be at home. The cottage was so small, and Mrs. Pattle and her family so large that Anne thought of the old woman who lived in a shoe whenever she looked at it; though Mrs. Pattle never seemed in any doubt what to do. She knew when to slap a child, and when only to swear at it.

No doubt she was a good mother, re-sembling very much one of the huge sows which sometimes wandered over the village green in front of her cottage—a sow whose steps were followed by a sounder of little porkers trotting about in all direc-tions. What if she did chastise one, or even gobble it up? One would not be missed. . . . No, indeed, for how did it come about that Mrs. Pattle had three children that all seemed to be between two and three years old, yet none of them twins? Was one of them Maggie's? Anne thought not, but it was difficult to be sure, and if the matter were not settled soon she would never know; on such points the Pattles' memories were not trustworthy. Yes, they were a slipshod family, though not exactly what one would call an immoral one. . . .

Yet, though Anne despised Maggie for her sluttishness and untruthfulness, in some ways she admired her. Maggie was a good girl, she did what she was told, had a passion for washing floors, and was not a bad cook. Then she would go anywhere at any time, and do anything for anybody to oblige. Mrs. Pattle's cottage was crawling with babies, could one of them be the fruit of this cheery good-nature?

But if Anne admired the way Maggie scrubbed the scullery floor, she felt envy when she saw her sauntering along the lanes with her hands in her pockets, whistling like a ploughboy, and stopping to speak to every person she met on the road. Did she envy Maggie only because she had so many friends, or was it partly because she knew all the boys and the young men, and went in the grove in the evenings, coming out with her cheeks no redder than they were by nature?

Why was it, Anne asked herself, that she could not whistle as she walked along in her long black dress and her black straw hat? She had no friends to talk to except the village people, and she could only visit them if they were ill, or in trouble. That, and watching her father feed the birds, was not enough to fill her life. She read, and when the young carters went ploughing she laid aside her book to watch them as they passed the house, sitting sideways on their great horses. Anne liked the way the men whistled, and their deep voices as they spoke to the cart-horses drinking at the pond, voices so full of restraint and kindliness. There was no way for her to speak to these young men who looked so cheerful as they went by to work in their rough clothes, though sometimes, when she was out on a long walk and was far from home, she had tried to get into conversation with a young farmer leaning over a gate, or with a gamekeeper idling along the edge of a wood, his black and white spaniel at his heels.

But the beds had to be made, and since she liked to sleep in a big four-poster that they had found in the vicarage on their arrival, and her father also slept in a large bed, she helped Maggie to turn the mattresses.

It takes two to make a bed properly, and with an unselfish companion who does not take more than her fair share of the sheets to tuck in on her side, it is pleasant work.

How the mattress bends and coils on itself, somersaulting heavily like a whale, and how brave the great linen sheet looks as you turn it down! The last of the two beds was made, and they were tucking in the quilt when a strange sound came from outside the house—a confused noise of voices singing. Was it a hymn?

" Whatever can that be, Maggie? " she asked.

" That's the carters come, Miss," the girl answered. " It is Plough Monday to-day."

" What is Plough Monday? "

Maggie could only stare at this question—she could not answer it, except by saying:

" Well, they always keep Plough Monday round here, though not properly, like they used to do. They came to the gate last year, but I told them not to come singing with your mother lying ill."

"I shall go and see," said Anne, and she ran across the landing from her bedroom, which faced the garden, into her father's, which overlooked the road.

Chapter 2

PLOUGH MONDAY

THE sound of voices came again, men and boys singing, one out of tune with the others, but all ringing with the same fresh gaiety and purity through the frosty air, reminding the hearer of the sharp notes of the blacksmith's hammer raining on the anvil, and giving him the same assurance that the very texture of man's ordinary life is a beautiful and joyous fabric.

This time Anne could hear the words of the song.

> One morning very early,
> The ploughboy he was seen
> All hastening to the stable
> His horses for to clean.

She ran to the window and, looking out into the whiteness, she was blinded for the first moment by the sun shining onto the dazzling field of snow, but in the next instant she perceived three great chestnut horses standing just below her immediately in front of the door. They were harnessed to a plough, at the handles of which stood a labourer, whilst at the head of each of the horses was a young carter, and on the foremost of the horses were two little boys riding. It was the voices of these little boys which were so oddly out of tune.

Anne was astonished to see them with their plough and horses so close to the doorstep, and was filled with a sense of strangeness even before she saw what was most strange about these visitors. That a plough should be standing so close to the house was strange, and even for the moment seemed to her shocking, for one of the horses was standing on a flower-bed, but this was nothing to the appearance of the men, for all of them had their faces blacked and their shoulders and their caps were white with snow. The black faces against the whiteness of the snow frightened her; for a moment she caught her breath with fear, which turned almost instantly to wonder and delight.

> With chaff and corn
> He did them bait,
> Their tails and manes
> He did comb straight.

What was it? What was it? Something strange, something beautiful, the thing

17   c

perhaps she had always wanted, and half guessed at, but which she had never before met face to face.

The tune changed:

> Come all you lads and lasses
> See a gay ploughboy.

Gay, yes, they were gay; the snow was falling, and the sun was shining, and they had blacked their faces and come to her doorstep, and one black face with an open pink mouth was looking up at her in the window.

> Please can you spare a halfpenny
> For an old ploughboy?
> A bit of bread and cheese
> Is better than nothing.

The song was over; one of the young carters came to the door and gave a knock which echoed through the house. Anne started, woken from her rapt contemplation of the horses and the men, and still repeating under her breath: " Beautiful, they are beautiful! " she ran downstairs to open the door. Mr. Dunnock, however, was there before her, and from the hall she could see nothing of the men with their black faces, nor of the plough, nor the horses with their satin coats, their manes flecked with snow, and their tails twisted up in plaits of straw; her father's back blocked the doorway, and she could hear his voice in anger.

"That's enough of this foolery. You should know better than to trample down the lawn and the flower-bed."

Give us a shilling and we shall be glad,
Give us a penny and we shall go home,

piped the two little boys from the horse's back. "Please, Sir, it's Plough Monday, we like to keep it up."

"I have nothing for you," said her father. "I have quite enough deserving objects for my charity." He shut the door, and found himself face to face with his daughter.

"Some village clod-hoppers have come begging," said the clergyman, throwing back his head and giving vent to a cough of irritation. "They actually brought three horses and a plough over the flower-beds and up to the door."

"They won't have hurt the flower-beds, father, in this weather, with so much snow on the ground," said Anne.

"Perhaps not," he answered, "but they have made a great mess of the snow in front of the house, besides I had wished to measure the footprints of the birds."

"You might have given them something, they seemed so jolly."

"Jolly?" Mr. Dunnock's cough became almost a bark. "It is not my idea of jollity, nor I should have hoped yours, for yokels to black their faces in imitation of Christie minstrels, and come begging for money simply because they are given a day's holiday on account of the weather."

"But, father, I think that it is an old custom, and that they expect to be given money."

Mr. Dunnock gazed at his daughter with real surprise.

"I won't hear of it. I most strongly disapprove. They may try other people. I am not going to be victimised, or imposed on. Old custom? Remember what the midshipman said in his letter to his mother: 'Manners they have none, and their customs are beastly.'" The clergyman recovered himself sufficiently to laugh at his own joke, but when his daughter moved towards the door, he said angrily: "I forbid you to encourage them, Anne;

the incident is closed and I have sent them away."

The local Christie minstrels, however, had not gone away, and as Mr. Dunnock spoke a loud knock resounded on the door.

"You had better go upstairs, Anne. Kindly leave me to deal with them."

Anne ran upstairs, trembling with rage, and rushed into her father's bedroom, where, by looking out of window, she was able to see what was going on and overhear most of what was being said.

When Mr. Dunnock opened the door he found all the ploughmen gathered in a group on the doorstep.

"It's Plough Monday, Sir, and we have come to keep it, and ask you for a piece of money for our song."

"I have told you already to go away," said the clergyman, coughing with exasperation. "I don't give money to beggars."

There was a silence, then one of the young men at the back laughed and said: "He doesn't tumble to it; tell the parson that it is Plough Monday."

"Where would you be if there weren't no ploughmen, or no ploughing done?" asked the spokesman of the group. "You wouldn't get no tithes if it weren't for the plough."

There was a chorus of approval at that.

" No, that you wouldn't! "

" He can't answer that, Fred."

They shouted, but at the word *tithes* Mr. Dunnock had slammed the door in their faces. The ploughmen knocked again, and for some minutes the sound echoed through every room in the house. Anne could see that they were puzzled, and in some doubt what to do next. One or two of them were laughing, another scratched his head while he said: " Called us beggars, did he? Reckon we work as hard as he." Presently they retreated to one corner of the garden and remained talking together for some little while, until Maggie appeared from round the corner of the kitchen and called out to them.

" You had best go away," she said. " The parson he says you are a lot of lazy louts. I heard him. He won't give you naught. You won't get nothing if you do plough his doorstep up."

The ploughmen did not answer her, nor did they appear to pay any attention to her words, but slowly went back to their horses' heads.

" What must be, must be," said the oldest of the company, laying hold of the handles of the plough. " I'ld as lief keep the custom. Come on, boys!" he shouted. At these words Anne could see that they all suddenly recovered their good humour, and a moment after they began joking among themselves.

" Parson will have to wipe his feet on his mat before we have done with him," said one lad.

" There won't be anyone shy of paying us our pennies after this," added another.

" Let him preach what sermon he likes next Sunday; there won't be no one but his daughter and our Maggie to hear him swearing."

" Hey, my beauties! " shouted the ploughman at the handles.

The great horses strained and began to move; the young carters at their heads shouted and led the team in a wide circle across the untouched snowfield which was the lawn; the plough sidled and circled through the snow, and the men began arguing with the horses.

" Hold back, can't you! "

" Steady there, whoa."

At last, after one horse had nearly put

23

its head through the window of Mr.
Dunnock's study, and another had trampled
down a rose bush, the plough was got
into position at the far corner of the house.
After that they all waited while the ploughman left the handles and began to hammer at part of his plough.

The fear which Anne had felt when she
first looked out returned to her, and the
sense of strangeness persisted. Was she
waking or dreaming, was she afraid or
was she glad? Suddenly she heard Maggie's voice saying in excited tones:

" You are never going to plough up
Mr. Dunnock's doorstep! " and hearing
these words Ann began to tremble.

At last the ploughman straightened
his back and said:

" Calls us idle beggars, does he? And
too busy to speak with us; we'll mark
Plough Monday in his prayer-book. Get
up there. . . ."

The horses strained, and the plough
sank through the snow into the soft earth
of a flower-bed, the traces tightened and
the three horses pulled; a wrinkle or two
showed itself in their haunches, and the
share of the plough threw up a broad
streak of raw earth.

24

" Steady, boys, steady by the door-step," called the ploughman, and the carters edged the horses nearer in to the wall of the house. In a moment the plough reached the door, and Anne, gazing down from above, saw the flagstone lift and topple, while the plough ran swiftly on, and the earth streamed out upon the snow.

" I must stop them," she whispered, but she did not move, or take her eyes off the scene. Watching from above, the girl was fascinated and horrified by every detail; the swift and irresistible progress of the hidden ploughshare running through the earth delighted her; the strength of the three stalwart Suffolk Punches, and the lean, sinewy wrists of the ploughman guiding the handles, and the gay young men, all thrilled her. While watching, she could not have told what were her emotions, yet she knew that the scene was beautiful; the plough slipping so easily in the rich earth had the grace and lissom strength of a snake. Once again the horses turned, sweeping down and halting beside the hedge of laurel, and there was another pause while the plough was got into position, and then the team swept round and strained forward again to cut the second furrow, and, that finished, to draw the plough out into the roadway in front of the vicarage, while the ploughman threw the handles on one side and held them down so that the share skidded through the snow over the grass.

The men did not call out, nor even appear to speak or to laugh among themselves; having cut their two furrows, they went away swiftly, pausing only for a moment on the road to adjust the ploughshare, and then hurrying on to sing their songs under other windows.

Only when the plough had turned the corner of the lane and the last of the horses' heads had vanished down the avenue of elm trees, did Anne Dunnock leave her position at the window, and only then did she burst into a flood of tears. " I cannot live after such an insult," she said to herself. " How could they do such a thing to our house? But why is it that it seemed to me so beautiful as well as so cruel? " and as she asked herself this question she noticed that though she had dried her tears her hands were still trembling. " The lawn of virgin snow has been torn up by the plough, the naked earth exposed, and the garden trampled over by the iron shoes of the horses and the hobnails of the labourers," she said. " And our doorstep has been overturned; my father's fault, for he was in the wrong. I feel now as if I could never forgive him for bringing this shame on us, yet if it had not been him it might have been me, for the same fault of character is in both of us. We are rejected everywhere, unable to share in the life around us, or to understand it. Enid taught me that at Ely, but to-day it has been recognized by the ploughmen, and this broad gash in the earth and the uprooted doorstep proclaim it to our neighbours. I shall never dare show my face in the village after this."

So saying, Anne Dunnock found herself sobbing again. " This is too silly," she told herself, yet the tears continued to flow, until she gave up resisting them and lay down on the bed in her own room. She thought of Enid, to whom she had written so many poems and so many passionate letters, only to discover that they had been shown to all the girls in the school, that they had been borrowed and read aloud in every bathroom where there were girls talking before going to bed. " I could have killed Enid; she made

27

all the girls in Ely think that I was perfectly ridiculous." And all the bitter experiences of her life came back into her mind and were confused with her present unhappiness.

" Why should we suffer from this? " she asked herself, after a few moments of weeping. " For I know father suffers from it as much as I do, though he has never spoken of it to me, and perhaps not even to himself. Is it because he is a clergyman, or is it because we are in some way superior, cleverer, or better than our neighbours? No," she answered herself, " it cannot be that, for though I am intelligent, perhaps even remarkably intelligent, father is terribly stupid. In fact he is almost deficient in some respects, and I am sure neither he nor I are superior morally. We are both too emotional and too ready to lose our tempers. All our troubles spring from the fact that father is a clergyman, for whether they recognize it or not, ordinary people have a contempt for the clergy, and clergymen are always ill at ease with their fellow men. Thank God father isn't one of the hearty sort; in his own way he is an honest man and a religious one, but he has ruined my life.

28

It is Ibsen's *Ghosts* over again," for Anne had been reading Ibsen lately. Then a phrase from another book she had been reading, De Quincey's *Opium-eater*, came into her mind: " Unwinding the accursed chain."

" How can I unwind the accursed chain? " she asked herself. " I must begin soon, for I am twenty-three, and the best part of my life is gone."

" It is no good crying over spilt milk," she said, and went on: " At all events I am glad that they did not go away when father told them to go; I am glad that they tore up our garden with that narrow snake-like plough wobbling a little as it ran through the earth. I am glad of it, though I shall find it hard to face our neighbours after this, for they will have changed. Everyone will know of our disgrace."

She rose from her bed and tidied her hair before the glass; as usual all the hairpins had fallen. Then turning to the window she looked out over the untouched snowfield at the back of the house where not even a dog had run as yet. Everything was covered, even the winter jessamine on the summer-house was concealed, and the black poplars beyond the pond had every twig laden with snow.

" All will be forgotten as soon as the snows are melted," she said to herself suddenly, with the certainty that her words were true. " All my emotion is nonsense. To me everything seems changed, but it is only a joke to the carters; they will laugh about it over a pint of beer to-day, but in a week's time they will have forgotten it; the fact that some dog has killed a rat will seem more important. My life is not changed: to-morrow the mason will come to lay the doorstep in its old place, and I shall say: ' It's a fine day,' when I go to the grocer's shop, and: ' Very seasonable weather,' when I take the loaves from the baker. That is the nearest that I shall ever get to contact with my fellows; why should they care how we live, what we do, or whether we disgrace ourselves or not? We mean nothing to them."

And Anne Dunnock, who only a few moments before had been weeping because the world was changed, began suddenly to weep again because it appeared to her that it had not changed and that it would always remain the same.

This time the tears were not so readily checked, for one tear brings the next after it, and Anne remained hidden in her bedroom until Maggie knocked at the door to say that lunch was on the table. But by then she herself had forgotten what had so much moved her less than two hours before, for she had taken up *Peer Gynt*, and as she went downstairs she was thinking not of the carters with their black faces and the snow on their caps, but of the trolls.

Chapter 3

SOTHEBY'S SHOP

IN the night the wind changed to the west and rain fell, so that by morning the snow was gone from the grass, and only lingered in a few places, on the roads and on the bare earth of the kitchen garden, and the rain which thawed the snow washed away the memory of Plough Monday, thus bringing to pass what Anne had fancied sooner than she had expected.

She no longer felt ashamed to go into the village, and as for her father, half an hour after the event he had forgotten his irritation in watching the starlings searching for worms in the loose earth thrown up by the plough.

After breakfast, old Noah, the gardener busied himself in filling in the furrow, and old Simmonds, who called himself a builder and fencing contractor, came round and, after mixing a little mortar on a board, laid the doorstep back, only a trifle askew, in its old place.

"There's your doorstep, Miss," he said, straightening his back as Anne opened the front door and stood on the threshold prepared for walking. " There's your doorstep; no one will ever shift that again."

Simmonds was right, for Anne lacked the courage to tell him to take it up and set it straight.

" May I step on it? " she asked.

" Aye, he'll bear your weight, Miss," said the old man blinking, and to prove his words he stepped onto the doorstep himself, blocking her path while he stamped once or twice with his hobnailed boots.

" Is that firm enough for you, Miss? " he asked, speaking with melancholy pride, and then standing aside for her to walk on it herself.

"Yes, that seems all right, Simmonds," she said, stepping onto the stone, and was aware as she spoke that her words were meaningless, for why should the old man be so proud of the force of gravity which kept the doorstep where it lay? Why should she have to give him credit for it?

"I was going to speak to your father, Miss, about the sills," said Simmonds.

" About what? "

" It's a long time since they were

33   D

painted, and the wood is perishing. I thought perhaps your father might like me to estimate for them."

Anne frowned; the question of the sills annoyed her, but she could not escape until she had looked at them.

Simmonds was right—the paint on the window-sills had cracked into hundreds of little grey lichenous cups.

" I'll speak to him about it," she said. " We must have it done one day."

The elm trees were so beautiful; it was because of the elms that she loved Dry Coulter. Soon the spring would come, soon the snowdrops would cluster thickly under the garden walls, and every day that passed improved the quality of the bird's song.

" There is no prison so terrible as beauty," she said suddenly to herself. " I love the seasons, the beauty of the village, the clouds, and the tall groves of elms standing round the green. I love our orchard with its old apple-trees, and the pears; I dream in the winter of what the crop will be in the following autumn, fearing that the bullfinches will take the buds, or the blossom be cut down by a late frost, yet time is flying—and while

34

my blood runs fast as it does now I must walk demurely like the old woman that I shall so soon become. Yes, I shall be old before I am free to live as I should like. Shall I ever go to the opera? A cheap seat would do—I cannot expect a box, or emeralds, but one can hear as well from the gallery, and it is the music that I want to hear. Shall I escape one day? Shall I go to London?"

Then it came into her mind that perhaps even if she went to London, even if she got to know interesting men (and such beings must exist), even if she went to the opera with them, she might still feel herself a prisoner, and that perhaps the most that one can do in life is to exchange one sort of beauty for another; the beauty of the apple trees for the beauty of music.

"Yes, there is no prison so terrible as beauty," she said again, and added immediately: "Now I must go to the grocer's," and though she disliked the grocer himself, she smiled with pleasure at the thought that she might see his little daughter Rachel.

"*Emmanuel Sotheby, Grocer and Provision Merchant*" was painted over the little shop with its windows filled with

bars of soap, packets of starch, clay pipes,
and walnuts, for Sotheby dealt in everything, and though the shop was small,
the stock was large. Sotheby always had
what you wanted: calico, mustard, cotton,
China tea, boot polish, even lamp chimneys. There was no shop so good as
Sotheby's in the nearest town: there was
nothing better than Sotheby's even in
Ely, yet would he be able to provide her
with drawing pins? It was unlikely, almost
impossible, and Anne determined not to
mention them until she had made her
other purchases; she would only speak
of them just before she left the shop. In
that way Mr. Sotheby would not feel
that she had expected too much of him,
or think that she was disappointed. With
her hand on the latch, she said to herself:
" I will not speak of the drawing pins if
there are other customers," but the shop
was empty, and the jangling bell brought
Mrs. Sotheby out of an inner room. The
grocer's wife was a slender woman of
fifty; her pale wrinkled face made her
seem older, though her hair was still a
beautiful brown, and when she smiled
she showed two even rows of little pearly
teeth. Mrs. Sotheby was always merry;

whenever Anne came into the shop her brown eyes twinkled, or she broke into a low musical laugh, while her face crumppled itself up into all its wrinkles, her white teeth flashed, and her eyes almost vanished. Such a merry laugh greeted Anne that morning, and Mrs. Sotheby explained it by a reference to the events of the day before.

" Good morning, Miss Dunnock, I have been hearing such dreadful things all yesterday about the ploughmen. I am afraid they must have upset your father, but you must not take any notice of them. It is all foolishness, and I don't know what the men can have been thinking of, but, of course, it is an old custom and they like keeping it on that account. You know men are just like boys about anything like that, but they did not mean to be disrespectful or unneighbourly, I'm sure. Your father is still rather a stranger here; I expect he did not understand their ways."

At Mrs. Sotheby's words Anne started, all her shame came back to her suddenly, but she saw that she must answer. A lump came in her throat, and her mouth trembled as she said:

"No, neither father nor I had ever heard of Plough Monday. It was entirely my father's fault: he is sometimes impatient when he is disturbed reading."

"It was very foolish of the men," said Mrs. Sotheby. "And they should feel ashamed of themselves, but directly I heard of it I knew there was a misunderstanding of some sort. It happens so easily, only I thought I would speak of it, because you know it is an old custom, and the men are proud of keeping it here, so you must make allowances for them."

The kindliness of these words was more than Anne could bear. "Thank you, thank you so much," she cried, and suddenly she found that her tears would flow—she could not keep them back, though she shook her head angrily, and as she did so a couple of hairpins dropped onto the floor.

At that moment a shadow passed in front of the windows; there was the sound of wheels, and a horse being pulled up short in front of the shop.

Anne looked about her wildly, but Mrs. Sotheby had lifted a flap of the counter and was saying:

"Come into our parlour and sit down

for a little while, Miss Dunnock; it was foolish of me to speak, but I never guessed you would have taken such nonsense to heart. If one were to pay attention to half the silly things men do, our lives would not be worth living."

Anne followed Mrs. Sotheby through the shop into a little room, with a coal fire burning in the grate. She sat down in the armchair pushed forward for her, while the grocer's wife hurried back into the shop, summoned by the jangling bell. For a little while Anne was overcome with mortification at finding herself in the grocer's parlour and wondered how she could have so disgraced herself.

Why, if she must cry every morning (and it seemed to have become a habit), could she not retire to her own room and weep in solitude? But after a few moments of humiliation the thought came into her mind that at last she had disgraced herself finally and for ever, and this reflection was a consolation to her.

" I cannot undo this. If I were to steal out of the back door without Mrs. Sotheby hearing me, it would make no difference. I have shown her my feelings; I have burst into tears in her shop; I cannot pretend to have any dignity after this."

Anne dried the last of her tears, reflecting that it was exciting to have made a fool of herself, and that if she had not lost her self-control she would never have been asked into that parlour. Then, taking off her hat, she began tidying her hair and looking about her.

The room she was in was small and richly furnished with uncomfortable armchairs, upholstered in dark red plush; there was a table covered with a red cloth, which had a fringe of little balls; a slowly ticking clock stood on the mantelpiece; on a small table, before the window, stood a large green pot containing an arum lily with one leaf half-unfurled and a white bud showing; from the curtain rod hung a wire cage full of maidenhair ferns. On the walls were photographs: Mr. and Mrs. Sotheby on their wedding day, a plump and rather ugly young woman, the Tower Bridge with a ship going through it, and a boy with pomatum on his hair. Then, turning her head, Anne saw a large photograph hanging just behind her.

"What a strange face!" for the young

man certainly had a strange face, and was wearing an odd little round cap, almost like a skull-cap, with a tiny tail sticking up in the middle; his throat was bare, with no sign of a collar or tie, or even of a shirt. A cigarette was hanging out of the corner of his mouth, but the strangest thing was not the cap, but the face, or rather the expression of the face, for the features themselves were vaguely familiar. The young man was laughing, but there was a look of careless contempt, almost of insolence, which Anne very much disliked. The nose was long and straight, and rather foxy, the eyes mere slits set wide apart; the forehead was broad and large, but the chin feeble. " Good gracious me! " exclaimed Anne, noticing that in one ear there was a little earring. "A man wearing an earring! How extraordinary!" She gazed at the photograph for some time, taking in every detail of the face. Certainly there was something disagreeable in the expression; the laughter was untrustworthy and heartless; he was laughing at other people, not sharing his laughter with them.

But the customer was staying a long while in the shop, and, becoming impatient, she went to the door and listened. The voice she heard was that of Mr. Lambert, a young farmer, whom Anne knew since he attended church (he was a church-warden), and once he had stopped her in the road and told her that she should go riding.

To Anne his remark had seemed ridiculous, since he must know well enough that they were too poor to keep a hack for her use, and he could not have meant that he had one for her to ride.

If he had wished to say: "If you get the habit, I'll mount you on one of my horses," why hadn't he said so? He could not have intended that, and even if he had, what would she have answered? What did he expect in return? That she should go riding with him? She smiled at the thought: Mr. Lambert's company might not be so bad, but she would not care for it if she were under an obligation to him. If she killed his horse in taking a fence . . . that would be awkward! And if he met a girl whom he liked better as a companion on his rides—in that case she would be left with the habit on her hands. Her father would never allow such a thing; think of the gossip there would be!

" Damn this place! Damn my father! "

she said to herself, and listening to the farmer's sharp, but very pleasant voice, and closing her eyes, she had for a moment the delicious sensation of the horse bounding under her, of patting its withers, listening to the creak of the saddle, and keeping her balance while she looked proudly over the level landscape of the fens.

"I will, I will, I will," she repeated to herself. "I will ride a horse once in my life. I will even if I get left with a riding habit. But I suppose that is the spirit which brings young girls to ruin. I can imagine how Maggie would say to herself: 'I will let my head be turned by a man, even if I am left with a baby.'" Anne laughed at the comparison. "Silly thoughts. . . . They hurry me on to absurdities, and all because Mr. Lambert said something polite and meaningless to me, for it is politeness to assume that one can do whatever one likes without regard for money. But here am I laughing when I ought still to be sobbing, since I am still waiting for Mrs. Sotheby to come and console me. What shall I do? How on earth, by what false pretences, did I ever get into this cosy little room? If Mr. Lambert does not go away soon, I shall

march into the shop, lift the flap in the
counter and go away."

She listened then to the voices. "Very
good, Mrs. Sotheby, you shall have the
pig for scalding on Thursday, unless Mr.
Sotheby sends me word to-morrow."

The bell of the shop tinkled; Mr. Lambert paused to add a last word, and Mrs.
Sotheby answered him: "Well, if you
say so, Mr. Lambert," and Anne could
hear her hand on the latch.

"Well, I thought Mr. Lambert was
never going. He had come to see Mr.
Sotheby about carting sand, and really I
didn't know what to say to him. Now I
have agreed to share a pig with him; let
me know if you would like a leg of pork,
or sausages, or one of my pork cheeses.
My husband is so busy now; I hardly see
him from morning till night; he is putting
up some cottages at Linton, and his mind
is far more on them than on the grocery
business, so that I have quite as much as
I can manage. I am really sorry that I
undertook to scald the pig, but it was
rather tempting. Still, however many
pigs I scald, I shall never do half so much
as Emmanuel does; he's out every day of
the week, and drives the round himself,

and then he preaches twice every Sunday,
here and in the Ebenezer Tabernacle at
Wet Coulter. Mr. Lambert wanted to see
him in a hurry, but I could not tell him
where to find my husband. I cannot keep
in my head half the things he is doing,
and I have not yet been out to see the
Linton cottages. Still, it keeps him in
good spirits, and he is doing it for my
boy. But I mustn't keep you any longer
now." Mrs. Sotheby stopped speaking,
she smiled, and added rather shyly: " You
will come and chat with me sometimes,
won't you, Miss Dunnock? "

Anne promised to come again soon,
and spoke of the Arum lily beginning to
unfold its flower, and then passing
through into the shop, asked for curry
powder and sultanas.

When these had been given her, she
hesitated, asking herself whether, after
Mrs. Sotheby's kindness, she could ask
for drawing-pins. Perhaps Mr. Sotheby
would fetch some from Linton, but at
that moment she felt shy of asking a man
who was building a row of cottages to
execute her little commissions. She would
wait until another day for that. But on
the doorstep she paused:

" Thank you for being so kind to me. I shall always come and talk to you if I am upset by anything."

The face behind the counter broke into hundreds of wrinkles, the little teeth shone, and a delighted laugh answered her. " Like pouring water out of a glass bottle," thought Anne as she went out into the winter sunshine.

There was happiness, who could doubt it? The secret of life was to be like the Sothebys, and to work as they did, absorbed in building cottages. Would she ever think the prospect of scalding a pig too tempting to be refused, if she were overworked already?

" Mr. Sotheby must be very enterprising," she said to herself, trying to conquer her dislike of him, and she forgot the grocer in gazing at the distant elms which bounded the far side of the village green a quarter of a mile away, for in the middle of the village was a long and lovely stretch of common pasture.

But who was the boy for whom Mr. Sotheby worked so hard? And Anne remembered that Maggie Pattle had once told her that the Sothebys had a son. Why was it that she had imagined that he was

46

dead? But it did not occur to her to connect him with the photograph in the parlour, for she was looking at the elm trees, and listening to the song of a thrush; then gazing at the roof of Lambert's barn, bathed in sunlight, she felt her heart beating happily, and asked herself why had she felt beauty was a prison? She could be happy in that village for ever, for spring was coming, and the birds were singing.

Chapter 4

THE TRAPEZE BOY

A HARD frost came early in February.

"If this lasts," said Mr. Dunnock eagerly, "we shall have skating the day after to-morrow," but his face clouded quickly, and he put down his cup with a gesture of annoyance. The day after to-morrow would be Sunday.

"We may be in for a long spell of frost," said Anne, but, reminded of his duties, her father was not in the mood to be consoled. "A frost brings more suffering than you or I can quite realise, my dear," he said severely. "Think of the poor, without the coal or the blankets to keep them warm; think of the seamen in the rigging of ships; think of the outcasts on the roads; think of the birds."

"Think of the polar bears," said Anne under her breath, as her father rose from the table and scooped out the crumb of the loaf.

"The trap ought to be here in ten minutes; I shall be back from Ely by the eight o'clock train," he said, and with these words went to the front door where

an impatient flock of sparrows was await-
ing his arrival.

When the trap came, she went to the
gate and watched her father drive away,
wondering whether he would meet Enid in
the street. "I am glad I am not going. Now
the rest of the day is mine. Mine, and I
am free to do whatever I choose! "

The road was like iron; it rang under
the pony's hoofs, and Anne thought she
had never seen a lovelier morning; the
spell of the frost was more beautiful than
the enchanted world of the snow had
been a month before, though it was not
so strange. Every twig was fledged with
rime, for there had been a fog during the
night, but already the sun had broken
through the mist, the sky was showing
blue overhead, and the white tops of the
elms were blushing in the sunshine.

" Every tree is smothered in snowy
blossom; it is as if spring had come," and
she thought that the flowering time of the
cherry in Japan could not equal the beauty
of this February morning in England.
When she turned to go back into the
house she noticed that the bare wall of the
vicarage was covered with hoarfrost, an
opalescent bloom shining in the sunlight.

" A fairy palace fit for the Snow Queen or the Sleeping Beauty," she said, and the words reminded her that Maggie must be waiting for her to make the beds.

" You ought to see the fat woman," said Maggie Pattle. " Her bosom was bigger than that pair of marrows Mr. Lambert gave for Harvest Festival; there's a paper outside says she is only twenty and weighs nineteen stone. I shall never call Ida Whalley fat again, after last night."

Linton Fair lasted two days, and the merry-go-rounds were staying till the end of the week.

" I went in the swing-boats, and I went to the circus, and I spent seven shillings altogether," said Maggie with triumph.

Anne shuddered at the fat woman, but when Maggie spoke of the circus, of the little lady who rode on a pink horse and jumped through paper hoops, and of a horse that undressed and went to bed and drew up the sheets with its teeth, she wished that she could go herself.

" Why not? Why not? " she wondered. " Why should I not go this afternoon? There is no disgrace in going to the fair, and there are the drawing-pins that I have to buy at Linton. I must begin trying to do some fashion plates. Besides, I should enjoy the walk on a day like this."

The six miles of road brought a glow of colour into her cheeks, and she felt her heart beat with excitement as she crossed the old bridge over the Ouse, and entered the little town. The streets were crowded with men and beasts; the market place was full of farmers and machinery, and half a dozen cheap-jacks, each surrounded by a dense crowd, were shouting against each other.

Anne quickened her pace; the noise of a steam organ told her that the merry-go-rounds were in a field near the railway station, but when she had passed the first booths, the cocoanut shies, the rifle-range, and the places where she was invited to win cups and saucers by throwing rings, she suddenly became embarrassed. Just in front of her were the swing-boats sure enough, laden with shrieking girls; beyond them a great merry-go-round painted with all the majesty of a heathen temple, and loaded with strange idols: swans, dolphins, lions, and ostriches, turned slowly round like a monstrous humming-top, and near-by was the vast curving canvas wall of the circus.

She was surrounded by a happy crowd, but she could not mingle with it.

Already her pink cheeks had drawn upon her the notice of a group of young farmers; it was clear to her that she could not visit the circus unless she went with a companion. At that moment she envied Maggie her freedom as she had never done before; Maggie, who might laugh or scream until her voice drowned the hurdy-gurdy, and who could answer back when a man spoke to her without anyone thinking the worse.

What would be said if she, Miss Dunnock, the daughter of the vicar of Dry Coulter, were to try to win a cocoa-nut? Many of her father's parishioners must be in town, and, with flagging footsteps, Anne passed by the entrance to the field full of merry-go-rounds, and walked slowly on towards the railway station.

Within the great tent of the circus she could hear the thumping of the ponies' hoofs, the crack of the circus-master's whip, and the falsetto note of a clown's voice, followed by a roar of rustic laughter and clapping hands; then, passing on, she came in view of the showmen's encampment: a score of caravans with smoking chimneys, groups of hobbled ponies, and women carrying pails of water, hanging out washing, and preparing the evening meal.

" A curious life," the girl said to herself. " Wandering from town to town, roaming from one country to another, for the circus I see here may be at Nizhni-novgorod next summer and in Italy or Spain six months after that. The women must have a hard life, but I would rather be one of them than the wife or daughter of a clergyman. If I were to join them; but that cannot be—some dark woman would stab me rather than have me for her daughter-in-law, yet if one of these handsome gipsies asked me, I would not hesitate to go with him. I would rather that my son were a clown or a lion-tamer than an archdeacon or a bishop."

Anne roused herself after a few minutes; the sun was setting, she felt chilly, and her thoughts had depressed her. "My mind runs in a circle," she said. "Whatever I see, whatever I do, I come back to the thought that I am an outcast unable to share in the life around me, or to enjoy it, and that somehow I must escape from my surroundings for I cannot live any longer without friends."

She turned back towards the market place, for there is nothing more gloomy than an empty railway station, resolving to buy what she needed and then go home without delay.

" Loneliness is terrible, and I have not got a friend in the world. The worst fate which can befall a human being is to be born a young lady," and meeting the gaze of a handsome gipsy with gold earrings, she added: " I can see that I do not attract him; he does not care for young ladies, and he is wise. We are an unhealthy, artificial breed; his women are better; they smell of tallow and wood ashes, and have the spirit and the health of mares."

Anne bought her drawing-pins and decided to go home, but first she would have a cup of tea, and threading her way past a steam plough with seven shares, and through a series of galvanised iron cisterns, at which a group of farmers were gazing with intellectual doubt written on their faces, she crossed the market place and went into White's. The turmoil of the fair had not penetrated inside the confectioner's shop, and she would have thought that they had no knowledge of it there if it were not that a greater primness reigned, and that the very gingerbread seemed weary of the flesh. Anne sipped her cup of tea with distaste, asking herself what the young ladies behind the counter would have said if she had given way to her desires, and they had seen her mounted on an ostrich. . . . Did they suffer from such temptations themselves?

She had almost finished her cup of tea when the door opened and a little girl came in, followed by a short thick-set white-bearded man of sixty. It was Rachel, her favourite, and her father, Mr. Sotheby. Rachel smiled, and all Anne's depression was laid aside, even the tea, tasting of wet boots, seemed changed by the pleasure of their meeting.

" Well, Rachel, have you been enjoying yourself at the fair? " she asked, looking into the pale little face, framed in short dark curls. The child nodded her head quickly.

" Yes, Miss Dunnock, thank you very much. I have been on the switchback, and enjoyed seeing the fair very much." Rachel's voice was always a trifle stilted, her words always polite, and her sentiments always perfectly correct, but Anne noticed that on this occasion the child's usual gaiety was lacking. A few words with the grocer were sufficent to explain the cause: Mr. Sotheby had brought Rachel into Linton to see the fair, he had taken her twice on the roundabout, but his business was waiting for him and must be done, and since he did not think it suitable to let the child go to the circus alone, he was leaving her at White's, where she would keep warm.

"Come and choose yourself a cake, Rachel," he said.

"May I take her to the circus, Mr. Sotheby?" asked Anne.

There could be no refusal, and the two friends set off at once, Rachel carrying the cheese-cake she had chosen, in her hand.

When the time came to meet Mr. Sotheby in the market place the two girls left the circus, and still under the spell of the wonders they had seen, it seemed as if they could never express sufficiently their admiration and their astonishment. The pink horse, and the fair rider of which Maggie had spoken that morning, and the clowns, who had appeared so suddenly that one might have thought a shower of frogs had fallen into the ring after a thunderstorm, were discussed in detail, but best of all, they had liked the handsome young man who had stood on his head on a trapeze, and who, without holding on with his hands, had swung rapidly from one side of the great roof of the circus to the other.

Mr. Sotheby was driving out of the inn-yard as they reached the market place, and Anne was about to say goodbye, when the grocer offered her a seat in his dogcart, saying that he would not hear of her walking back alone. She was grateful for his offer, for she had no great fancy for the six-mile walk herself, and soon they were all ready, tucked up in a large rug, with nothing to be seen of Rachel, crouching against their legs, but the tassel of her woollen cap. Mr. Sotheby flicked the pony with his whip, and in a few moments they had crossed the old bridge over the river, and had left Linton behind.

During the drive home, Anne's thoughts ran on the young man, dressed in scarlet tights like Mephistopheles, she could not forget his proud and serious face, intent only on his trapeze and indifferent to the audience; she would never forget that un-smiling face, looking up at the trapeze above him, as he deliberately rubbed first the soles of his shoes, and then his hands, in a box of sand.

But she could not speak of the young man, or of the circus, to Mr. Sotheby, whom she disliked; she could not continue her happy talk with Rachel in front of him, and they drove in silence—a silence broken at last by the grocer remarking on the number of foreigners that there were at the fair.

" Nothing interests us country folk more than to see a foreigner," said he. " A black man will draw a crowd anywhere, and no wonder either, for however contented we may be with our own lives, we always wish to learn about those of other people."

" He is a foreigner, of course," Anne was saying to herself. " Perhaps if I went to the circus again to-morrow I might learn his name, and whether he is an Italian or a Spaniard," but she roused herself, for Mr. Sotheby was still speaking, and then, wondering whether his words required an answer, she looked about her.

The risen moon was nearly full: there were no stars, and the road before them sparkled with frost. " How fast we are driving," she reflected. " There is nothing like a frost to make a pony go, and no doubt he is thinking of his stable." The sound of the hoofs rang out; the air was much colder than in the morning, so cold that it hurt her to breathe.

" My son Richard is abroad, living in Paris," said the grocer, and hearing his voice, Anne told herself that politeness required her to listen. If she married the trapezist she might live in Paris, too—or else they would travel from town to town wherever there were circuses.

" Before that boy was eight years old," Mr. Sotheby went on, " I knew that he would have to be a gentleman, and I am proud to say that I always encouraged him to do what he wanted with his life."

She would call him Lorenzo. What did it matter whether Lorenzo was a gentleman or not? And Anne said this to herself, certain that the boy who had swung so gracefully on the trapeze was a gentleman. " For what is gentility but pride and perfect dignity? And he is as proud as Lucifer."

" Everyone says that I spoil Richard," and the old man beside her cracked his whip gaily. " But as long as I can make money I shall send it to him."

" I am sure you are quite right," said Anne. Money! If only she had a little money! How that would simplify things!

Mr. Sotheby had needed no encouragement, and went on speaking: " All these farmers hoard their money, and laugh at me for spending mine, but I always say that we are both in the right, for they haven't sons like my Richard. What good is money to my wife and me? " he asked, but, without waiting for a reply, continued: " To him it means books, education, painting in the best studios, and the company of his equals, for he would not find his equals about here."

" Yes, money means all that and more," thought Anne, but aloud she said:

" Is Lorenzo a painter, then? "

" My son Richard? No, he is an artist. I am fond of pictures myself, so I can understand him. I have seen some by the great men: Rembrandt, Turner, and Wouverman. There is a fine gallery at Norwich."

" I am very fond of pictures, too," said Anne. " I have always wanted to try oils; perhaps I shall one day."

" I thought at first of sending Richard to Cambridge," said the grocer, for he was not interested in Anne's chances of painting. " But he said no to it. ' There's only one place where I can learn to be an artist,' he said. 'Paris is the only place for that.' "

Mr. Sotheby shook the reins, and murmured to his pony as they crossed a little bridge, then he continued:" One hears a great deal about the wickedness of Paris; several of our ministers have spoken to me about it, but I console myself with thinking that none of those men would mind letting their boys go to sea, and there is as much wickedness in Hull or Swansea as anywhere on earth."

Rachel shifted her position under the rug, and suddenly thrusting her head out, looked about her with curiosity, like a little monkey.

" Do sailors believe in the Pope of Rome, father? " she asked in her precise voice.

Anne did not listen to the reply. Of course Lorenzo was a Roman Catholic. Her father would be heartbroken, but she would give up everything for Lorenzo. Together they would voyage over the roads of Europe, their horses trotting on through the night, while the van they were sleeping in rocked gently on its springs. In the early morning she would wake to find that they were encamped by the side of a stream; the curling smoke of the wood fire would be rising beneath an ash tree; and near at hand the piebald horses would be hobbled, and happily grazing on the dew-soaked grass. She would wander along the hedge-row, startling a wood pigeon which would rise from the cornfield, and catching sight of the black and white of a magpie stealing along the edge of the wood. Soon she would return with her arms full of dog-roses, and would give one to Lorenzo to wear in his buttonhole; and in the evening she would see the fragile flower pinned to his breast as he swung on the trapeze.

" Scripture tells us," said Mr. Sotheby, " that children should honour their parents, but I feel a respect for my son which I never felt for my father, and which I don't expect Richard to feel for me. I know that he works as hard at his painting as I should expect him to work if he had stayed in the shop, though of course he earns no money by it. Perhaps he never will, for the qualities necessary are not the same, and Richard has spoken of men as great as Wouverman, living and painting in Paris to-day, who cannot sell their pictures. I would rather that Richard were to become a great master than that he were to sell a picture for hundreds of guineas, and incur the contempt of such men. Money is not everything: one need only read one's Bible to see that."

The pony slackened its speed, and turned a corner; they were back at Dry Coulter.

" Steady, boy," said the grocer, pulling up at the vicarage gate.

" Thank you very much, Mr. Sotheby," said Anne.

" A pleasure, Miss Dunnock; thank you for taking Rachel to the circus."

" Good-night, Mr. Sotheby. Good-night, Rachel."

" Good-night, Miss Dunnock, thank you for your kindness," came the child's voice as the pony darted off impatiently.

" What a glorious moon," Anne said to herself. " And what a hard frost! There will be skating without a doubt." She would like to have gone for a long walk to straighten out her tangled feelings, but it was half-past seven: it was time to lay the table for dinner.

"Perhaps Lorenzo is married," she said to herself suddenly. "Then we can only be friends," she added as she opened the door.

Chapter 5

THE FROST HELD

T H E frost held. On Sunday morning the little boys lingered round the edges of the Broad Ditch on their way to chapel, and Mr. Dunnock, hurrying to the vestry, noticed Mr. Lambert's foxhound puppy running across the ice.

"There will be skating," he said to himself, "and I have not lived all my life in the fens for nothing. I can still show the younger men something," and he decided to ask Anne to cut sandwiches. They would spend the morrow at Bluntisham:—a long walk, but one which would repay them with the finest stretch of ice in Huntingdonshire, and at Bluntisham Mr. Dunnock would see the best figure skaters and be seen by them.

After evening service he tapped the barometer, asking himself if it would be tempting Providence if he were to look at the skates that evening. There might be a screw missing, a strap needed, or a broken bootlace, and such little things were best attended to overnight, he reflected, trying to conceal his eagerness, for he would not be happy until he had handled his skates.

" They will be in the box-room," he said, taking a candle with him from the hall, but in the box-room many things met his eye which reminded him of his life at Ely. It had been a wretched subordinate existence, supporting his wife and daughter on a hundred and twenty pounds a year, but as he looked back on it such things were forgotten, and it seemed to him that his life there had been a happy one, for it had been shared with the woman he loved. Setting down his candle, he turned over the Japanese screen, which he had always liked for the storks flying across it, embroidered in silver thread. His wife had intended to re-cover the screen, for the storks were tarnished, and the silver threads unravelling, but she had died before she had found a suitable piece of stuff. " She is in Heaven," he said mechanically, and was surprised once again that the words with which he comforted others held no consolation for him.

" An old age passed together would have brought a closer understanding between us," he said, suddenly speaking

66

his innermost thought, which he had not admitted to himself before, for the clergyman's tragedy was never to have had the conviction of perfect understanding or intimacy, even with his wife.

" In the middle years of life we live too much in the affairs of the day, and a child troubles the mind of its mother. So many burdens to be borne, so many duties to be fulfilled. . . . We were too occupied to look into each other's hearts, and old age, the sweetest portion of life if it be filled with harmony, and the happiness of memories shared in common, old age is reserved for me only; a lonely and miserable old age. Now that I have lost Mavis, intimacy is impossible with anyone else, and I feel myself growing far away from everyone, and farthest of all from Anne. She reminds me too closely of her mother; I find it painful to be with her and I find her youth as tiresome as she finds my hasty temper."

Mr. Dunnock told himself that such feelings must be controlled, but he had said that before, and had no faith that the strangeness which seemed to be growing upon him, could be overcome. " Death will release me, and I must console myself with the hope that Mavis is waiting for me in Heaven, that she will fold me in her wings, and take me to herself without a word of reproach. When I hear the birds singing in the mornings they repeat that promise, and once or twice I have had the conviction that when I looked out of our bedroom window I should see angels perched in the branches of the trees."

The three pairs of skates lay on a shelf, the blades had been smeared with vaseline and wrapped in greaseproof paper, but the boots were dusty, and stretched stiffly over the boxwood trees.

" Yes, yes, the skates will be all right: there will be nothing amiss with them," for they had been greased by *her* hands; it was *she* who had laid them aside after the frost last winter a few weeks before her death.

The road to Bluntisham was long, and, as she walked with her father, Anne thought about bicycles. Her father had once had a bicycle, but that was many years ago; he appeared to have no wish to possess another, and Anne had never summoned up sufficient courage to buy one for herself, though the price of a bicycle was lying idly in the savings bank at the Post Office.

"I shall certainly buy a bicycle," she thought. "It is madness not to have got one before; a bicycle would give me the freedom for which I pine; what the horse is to the Arab of the desert, a bicycle is to a girl in my position. I could ride to Cambridge; in Cambridge I could go to concerts, and even plays; I could ride to Peterborough." But she did not finish her thought, for she was uncertain what Peterborough would give her.

"If I had a bicycle I should make friends and instead of wasting my life like a fool, dreaming about acrobats at a travelling circus, I should meet Cambridge undergraduates, and receive invitations to play tennis, or to join in a picnic party on the river."

While Anne was thinking of all the changes which would come into her life when she bought herself a bicycle, her father was enjoying the exercise of walking.

"I am a great pedestrian," he had said to the Bishop, and although he scarcely ever went outside his house if he could avoid it, the saying was true, and it was all his daughter could do to keep up with him.

Bluntisham church stands as the last outpost over the flooded fen country; a little beyond, at Earith, is the starting point of the Bedford Level which runs for thirty miles to King's Lynn without a hedge, or a tree, or even as much as a mole-hill to break the flat expanse—green all the summer, but under water, or rather under ice, when the Dunnocks approached it.

The father and daughter had in common a great liking for the fens; they loved the black peaty earth, the vast level expanse of sodden land, which looked flatter than the sea, when viewed from the high banks of a causeway running through it, or the embankments of the Bedford River raised up above the fields which it drained; they liked even the squalid villages on each side of the level, the low houses clustering wherever a hillock projecting into the fenland made it possible for man to build. But better than the Bedford Level of the present day, they loved to think of the fens of the past, and of the struggle to reclaim them, which had begun with the war between the Romans and the Iceni, flitting from islet to islet in their osier coracles, sheltering behind the willows, and making a night attack on the legionaries posted to defend the bridge at Huntingdon.

As they drew near Bluntisham they began to speak of these things, and Mr. Dunnock soon passed from the invasions of the Danes to the prosperous farmers who tilled the lands reclaimed by the Romans until the twelfth or fourteenth century when the fields relapsed into fenland, and soon they reached the great days of the seventeenth century, for, as Mr. Dunnock said, the history of the Commonwealth is to be found in the Fens of Huntingdonshire, and the Commonwealth itself may be regarded as a mere episode in the struggle between the Uplanders and the Lowlanders.

Although Mr. Dunnock was an Uplander by birth, and a High Churchman, he was proud of the part that the inhabitants of the swamps had played in English History.

"Without the three men of Godmanchester there would have been no Magna Charta, and if Charles had not tried to drain the Fens, there is little doubt he would have won the Civil War," he said, and went on telling Anne how as a young man Oliver must have made the reflection that his family had been ruined by the Stuarts who had encouraged their hopes and given them nothing. It was a good reason for him to repent of his loose life, and become more determined a Puritan. Soon he was stirring up trouble against the church in St. Ives; then his uncle, Sir Thomas Steward, died, leaving him his heir, and Oliver removed to Ely, but the temptation to make trouble still persisted, and when one next hears of him he was giving money to the Fen Dwellers and helping them to resist the drainage schemes of the King's Adventurers.

"Adventurers' Fen is called after them," said Anne, and her father answered that it might well be so, and they stopped for a moment to look out towards the fen in question.

"At that time the people in the fens lived by fishing and wild fowling," said Mr. Dunnock. "Every week during the winter a train of waggons left Linton for London loaded with wild duck," and he continued his story of how when the King was engaged in reclaiming the fen, the birds were driven from their nesting grounds, and the great decoys woven of

72

osiers were being left high and dry, so
that the lowlanders foresaw that they
would have to abandon a mode of liveli-
hood which had endured since the Iceni.
They had no desire to plough and reap,
and the drained lands did not prove fertile
until a century afterwards, when the
farmers were shown how to dig through
the peat and quarry clay to mix with it,
after which it became the most fruitful
soil in England. Oliver Cromwell had
taken up their cause, and later, when the
Duke of Manchester was letting victory
slip out of the hands of the Parliament,
it was Cromwell who impeached him, and
then seeking an army, turned for his New
Model to the Fens. It was Cromwell who
equipped the Lowlanders, and headed the
Eastern Association, and it was the Eastern
Association which had won the Civil
War, and so the Cromwells had their
revenge on the Stuarts. But though the
lowlanders had been made use of, the
work of drainage went on, and the Ironsides who had been enlisted to resist the
draining of the fens, were betrayed by
old Ironsides himself, the Lord Protector.

But by the time Mr. Dunnock had
reached this crowning example of the

perfidy of the figure he so much hated, they had turned the corner below Bluntisham Church, and saw before them the great expanse of ice covered with the descendants of Cromwell's Ironsides.

The field beside the road was full of motor-cars, of farmers' gigs, waggonettes, and grazing ponies, and at the entrance stood the farmer asking a penny from every person who went on the ice. No crop had ever yielded so handsome a profit as his flooded water-meadows, and no fenman in Cromwell's day would have fought more bitterly against a scheme which would have kept it drained during the winter months.

The noise of hundreds of pairs of skates on the ice came to their ears as they entered the field,—a grumbling sound that had within it a note which rang as clear as a bell, and they sat down to unlace their boots, refusing the offer of a chair which would mean spending another penny.

Anne was the first on the ice, and as her father watched her hesitating strokes the feeling of affection, which the conversation about Cromwell had aroused, gave place to one of shame and irritation.

" Am I to be tied to such a limpet all

day? " he asked himself as he had so often asked himself before when skating with his wife; then, without giving his daughter another look, he hobbled rapidly to the edge of the ice and was off himself, slipping away as easily as a swallow that recovers the freedom of its element after beating against the window-panes. His own strokes were as effortless as the flicking of a bird's wing, and it was impossible for the onlookers watching him to say what kept him in motion. Mr Dunnock never appeared to strike off, but leant gracefully forward, lifting a leg slightly to cross his feet, and changing his weight from one leg to the other, he flew lazily across the ice, picking his way without appearing to observe the existence of the clumsy young farmers who doubled up, and, with their hands clasped behind their backs, dashed round and round at top speed on their long fen skates. Soon everyone had noticed the tall clergyman with his beard tucked under a white woollen muffler, and many paused to watch as he began figure-skating in the real English style. Eight after eight was drawn with the slow precision of a sleepy rook wheeling in the evening sky, before descending in a perfect spiral to roost on the topmost bough of the high elm, and indeed the black-coated figure forgot for a few moments that he was an elderly vicar on a pair of skates, and believed himself to be circling in space among a vast flock of waterfowl flying over the fens. It seemed to him as if at intervals a V-shaped band of wild duck flashed past him, each with its neck craned forward, and beating furiously with its short, clumsy wings; a flock of curlew was all about him, and would wheel suddenly in its tracks with a flash of white, then a stray snipe corkscrewed past, a pair of greedy seagulls chased each other, and two roseate terns revolved round each other on their nuptial flight. . . .

Half an hour had gone by when his dream was interrupted by a young man with pink cheeks and rather protruding black eyes, who skated up to him and addressed him by name. It was Dr. Yockney, Dr. Boulder's assistant, whose professional duties brought him to Dry Coulter when there was a birth, or death, but rarely at other times:—the villagers were uncommonly healthy, and on the rare occasions when they took cold, or developed inflammation of the lungs, they doctored each other with gaseous mixture, or turpentine and honey.

"Ah, so you are here," said Mr. Dunnock shaking hands warmly, for young Yockney had attended Mrs. Dunnock in her last illness, and his sympathy and tenderness to the dying woman would never be forgotten.

"Yes, Doctor Boulder gave me the day off. This frost is so healthy we have no patients left; but it's an ill-wind that blows nobody any good, and I would not miss a day's skating like this for the world."

Mr. Dunnock said that Doctor Boulder must write to the Clerk of the Weather about the deplorably healthy winter. Mr. Yockney laughed, and then both of them remembered that it must be lunch time.

"Come, Yockney, you must join us," said Mr. Dunnock, and Anne coming up at that moment added her invitation, which the young man was glad enough to accept.

A line of trestles had been put up on the ice, and crowds were waiting round the shoemaker's, and the men who let out skates for hire, but most popular of all were the sellers of hot potatoes and roast chestnuts with their buckets of glowing coals. Mr. Yockney purchased three steaming cups of cocoa, while Anne went to fetch the satchel full of sandwiches, and in a little while they were sitting on the edge of a grassy bank.

" I have been seeing a friend of yours, Miss Dunnock," said the doctor after the second sandwich. " Little Rachel Sotheby, and I fear that it may have been your doing that I had to be called in, for I understand it was you who took her to the circus. She caught a chill on the way back. Oh, no, it is nothing in the least serious, though she is rather delicate."

Anne expressed her concern, and hastened to explain to her father how she had met the Sothebys in the tea-shop, and had taken the little girl to see the circus.

" Extraordinary chap that old grocer is," said Mr. Yockney. " He'd have been a rich man by now, I fancy, if it had not been for that good-for-nothing son of his. Just fancy, he told me that he was spending all his money on making his son a gentleman! "

This seemed to Mr. Dunnock an excellent joke, and he laughed heartily. He disliked the grocer for his assurance, and

78

his cheerfulness, and his nonconformity, and was ready to hear anything to his disadvantage.

" The great news," continued Mr. Yockney, " only I expect you know it, is that the prodigal is expected home next week. He's been in Paris, and has been going the pace a bit I fancy."

" Oh, I am so glad," said Anne with real interest showing in her voice. " I have heard so much about him from Mr. Sotheby, and I quite look forward to seeing what he's like. He sounds quite an interesting person."

A frown gathered on her father's face.

" Yes, we are all eager to see him," said the doctor, and then the tone of his voice changed so completely that Anne could see that it was another, and a serious Mr. Yockney who was speaking, although she observed that his eyes bulged just as much when he was serious as when he was only talking lightly.

" If you ask me, Miss Dunnock, I should say that young man is the very worst type of rotter. Look at the old grocer sweating away at sixty, look at his mother still serving in the shop, look at his little sister with patches on the sides of her boots, while Master Richard is learning to be a *gentleman* in Paris! There's no word too bad for him, I should like him to know what decent people think of that sort of gentility!"

"You had better tell him, my dear fellow," said Mr. Dunnock languidly. "It would do him a world of good, I've no doubt. But I must say it is probably not the fault of the son but because of the vanity of the father. Over and over again I have seen a young oaf of that description produced by a couple of vain and silly parents, who ruin their children's lives by denying them nothing."

"But no decent chap, you must admit . . ." said Mr. Yockney.

"You think the son is to blame because you are nearer his age and imagine yourself in his position," said Mr. Dunnock with a smile. "But I, as a father, imagine myself in the position of our excellent grocer. If I were to bring Anne up to expect luxuries, and to suppose that she was born to lead an idle, useless existence, it would not be her fault if she grew up a silly and discontented woman."

Even without this argument Anne was feeling decidedly uncomfortable, and a

clumsy piece of gallantry from Mr. Yockney added to her irritation.

"Stupid, coarse, hidebound brute! Do
your eyes bulge because of your manly
virtue?" she said under her breath, but
she had to confess that there was something in what the doctor had said. She
had not noticed the patches on Rachel's
boots herself, and she felt her respect for
Mr. Yockney as a doctor increasing with
her dislike of him as a man. If it were true,
it was disgraceful that Rachel should not
have a sound pair of boots, but it was
absurd to object to Mrs. Sotheby serving
in the shop; would she have been happier
at a hydro in Harrogate?

Mr. Dunnock had continued a whim-
sical description of how he might have
brought up his daughter so that she would
have been discontented with her life; the
doctor replied, but finally they agreed
that both of the Sothebys, father and son,
were very much to blame, when Anne
remarked in a voice which trembled, that
she was fond of the Sothebys and that
she thought that it was very fine of them
to sacrifice themselves in order to make
their son a great artist.

"I can trust you not to be taken in by

the word *gentleman*, Anne, but I am afraid you may be by the word *artist*. Art, you know, Mr. Yockney, covers a multitude of sins."

" The best definition of art I have ever heard," said the doctor, " is that it is the opposite of work." Mr. Dunnock laughed approvingly, and Mr. Yockney went on, his eyes bulging more than ever with the seriousness of his appeal.

" No, Miss Dunnock, whatever you may say, I know that the kind of caddish selfishness we have been talking about is absolutely abhorrent to you, as it is to all decent people. I quite agree with you that there is something pathetic in the old Sothebys, but there is nothing to be said for the son."

" Well, they seem to be an unusually happy family," answered Anne, feeling that she had lost her temper.

"I am too old to play at Happy Families any longer," said her father with a titter. " I shall go back to the ice and leave Mr. Yockney and you to settle the momentous question of Master Grits the Grocer's son."

Chapter 6

WINGED SEEDS

" Why is it? " Anne Dunnock asked herself next day, " that my father can be pleasant to other people but not to me? Though to be sure I fancied yesterday that his pleasantness to Mr. Yockney was a trifle vulgar, while his unpleasantness to me has at all events the merit of being sincere and well-bred." And Anne told herself that the only explanation must be that she was as much a burden to her father as he was to her. " But only I realise it," she burst out. " For I am young enough to recognise the truth, and to welcome it; he does not understand himself or other people; all his life he has hidden his head in the sand like an ostrich, and after all what else can one expect of a clergyman? "

Her anger had lasted since the conversation about the Sothebys, for her irritation during the lunch beside the ice had been quickly followed by fatigue which had intensified her resentment. After the unaccustomed exercise her ankles seemed to have turned to jelly,

83

and the eight-mile walk from Bluntisham had been torture to her.

"Never again," she said to herself; and when Mr. Lambert had stopped at the door next morning to offer her a place in his gig (he was going to Bluntisham for the skating), she had refused, and her father had accepted in her place.

"If I want any skating I shall go on the Broad Ditch," she had said, a remark which had estranged Mr. Dunnock more than her sullenness the previous day had done, and he drove off with a hurt look which said: "You are no daughter of mine to speak of skating in such a way before a stranger!"

When the gig was out of sight Anne went indoors to write a letter to Coventry for a catalogue of bicycles.

The catalogue came, but though she selected a machine, she hesitated to post the letter ordering it, and after a week's indecision, she tore it up, since the thought had come to her that a bicycle would tie her more firmly than ever to her life with her father, and this life seemed every day to become less endurable.

A thaw followed quickly on the second day of skating, and after that rain and sleet fell for several days. Mr. Dunnock appeared to be equally disgusted by the weather and by his daughter, and retired to his study, scarcely a word being exchanged throughout the day except at breakfast, when Mr. Dunnock always reminded Anne of her duties in the parish.

" A bicycle would rivet me to my present life," said Anne to herself. " What a chain is to a yard-dog, a bicycle is to the daughter of a clergyman! A bicycle would give me a certain radius of movement; it would fill the emptiness of my life; but I want things that no bicycle can give me. Yes, I want books, music, beautiful clothes, and more than any of these I want what they stand for, that is the society of intelligent men and cultivated women. Such hopes are vain I know: I shall never succeed in 'unwinding the accursed chain '—still I shall attempt it and the best way to set about it is certainly not by entangling myself with a bicycle. Even if I had to live in solitude I should prefer independence, and that I can achieve, for the world is full of women who earn their own living. Ten pounds is more valuable to me than a machine with plated rims or a little oil-bath; no one ever ran away from home on a bicycle, and I shall want all my savings for a railway ticket and lodgings in London while I look about me."

So the letter ordering the bicycle was torn up, and the catalogue itself cast into the fire, since it was a temptation to the flesh, one which assailed her particularly in the evenings; the ten pounds was replaced to her credit in the Savings Bank, and several days were spent in turning over the best way of earning her living.

"I shall go away from here, that is clear," she said. "I have known that ever since the ploughmen came that snowy morning. Here the accursed chain can never be unwound, but when I am living a free life, among new people, and my father is forgotten, I shall escape, and speaking easily to everyone I shall be accepted by them; I shall love; I shall be beloved. . . ." Anne shook her head and a shower of hairpins flew out onto the floor.

"Damn the elastic stuff!" she cried. "Why do I endure it a moment longer?" and, tears coming into her eyes, she started up and seized a pair of scissors out of her workbasket.

" There will be time enough for that later on," and the scissors were dropped as she told herself that she must plan for the future, and not dissipate her emotions in the present.

Yet another week was spent in considering how she could earn her living, and March came in like a lamb before she had arrived at any practical decision.

" The birds sing and build their nests, soon they will be laying their eggs, and then father will be in agonies whenever a young thrush hops across the lawn, lest it should fall between Pussy's paws. The snowdrops are over long ago, the hyacinths have broken through the ground, their fat buds look like pine-cones. First came the daffodils, the double ones, and then the single. The peaches are showing their pink petals on the walls of the dove-house, but I remain where I am, I cannot flower, unfold my petals or spread my wings. . . ."

When her father spoke to her of the migrant birds flitting northwards through Africa and Spain and Italy and France, from bush to bush, twenty yards by twenty yards, to find their way to England's shores " where alone they find the

87

happiness of love," said Mr. Dunnock, " and where alone they sing," Anne vowed fiercely that before the last of the migrants arrived she would be gone herself.

" The cuckoo will be here in six weeks," said she to herself. " The nightingale will be here a week after; I shall stay to hear one but not the other. Which it will be I cannot tell, for sometimes the nightingale comes before the cuckoo, and that they say is the luckier. I hope I shall hear the nightingale before I go and not the cuckoo; it would be an omen that I should find a true lover waiting for me, and not a deceiver."

The spring pleased her and excited her, and an hour or two was spent happily searching for the first wild flowers, and gathering the sweet-scented white violets which grew under the old apple trees, but meeting her father at lunch and hearing him speak to her of the Sunday school reminded her of her resolution to leave him, and at that moment the beauty of the springtime seemed nothing but a reflection of the weakness of her character.

" How can I leave him? He is helpless, and I am useful to him. Who will teach in the Sunday school? Who will keep up the thin pretence that he cares what happens to his parishioners when I am gone? Without me who will order his meals, and who will keep a watch on the bacon? The Pattles will rob him; they will eat him out of house and home." But though it seemed that it was impossible for her to leave her father helpless, and though Anne knew that she loved him, she was soon going over her old arguments about how a girl can earn her living.

All her experiences had been no more than to pour out tea, and to teach in the Sunday school. Other women of her age she knew were able to be bank clerks, or the secretaries of business men, they worked in Government offices, they did typewriting, indeed there seemed nothing that women did not do, but Anne doubted very much whether she could become a useful person of that kind. She had received what Mr. Dunnock had called " the education of a lady " (that was no education at all), she could not add up columns of figures, or use a typewriter, or write in shorthand. All she could do was to keep the children quiet, to tell them Bible stories about Balaam's ass, and Daniel in the den of lions; she could order the groceries, check the washing, arrange a bowl of flowers, speak boarding-school French and struggle somehow through a piece of Schumann—letting the hammer notes sound rather weak as her fingers tired.

To earn her living seemed impossible unless she were to succeed with her fashion plates, or were to exchange one Sunday school for another. That was always possible, and in another parish she would meet with a curate who would ask her to marry him, for nowhere could a curate find a better wife.

"Better a bicycle than a curate!" she exclaimed. "I would rather cut my throat than be the wife of a clergyman. Other duties perhaps I might face, but I have not the courage to work all my life for parishioners who prefer to go to their own chapels, or to the public-house. It is the fashion plates or suicide."

But then Anne remembered that there were many elderly ladies in the world, whose incomes permitted the keeping of a donkey-carriage, with a companion to walk beside it. "Why should I not be such a companion?" she asked. "In the

winter her sciatica will require a change of
climate, and we shall go away together to
the Riviera, or to Egypt." And the rest
of the afternoon was spent dreaming of the
music she would be hearing at Rome, of
seeing the Sphinx by moonlight and visit-
ing Tutankhamen's grave.

By the evening she had decided to put
an advertisement in *The Church Times*, and
at night she lay awake repeating to herself
the magic words which would bring her
freedom: " A well-educated girl, daughter of a clergyman, requires situation as
companion to a lady of means." No, that
did not sound well: should she call herself
" a respectable girl "? No, not a respectable girl—that smacked of the kitchen.
" A quiet girl, with an old-fashioned
education, desires to become the paid
companion of a lady." Nothing would
do, but nevertheless the advertisement
would have to be sent, and finding sleep
impossible, Anne took pen and paper and
wrote first one sentence and then another
until she had covered several sheets.

Next morning all her efforts seemed in
vain, but at last she decided on sending
the sentence which seemed to her to be
the clearest. " Young lady, who has en-

joyed a religious upbringing, wishes to see the world as the paid companion of a lady." There was nothing more required but a covering letter to the newspaper, and a postal order.

Anne put on her boots and hurried out into the blustering March wind. It had broken the first hyacinth, and the daffodils were lying flat on the earth. How the wind roared! It was pleasant to be out of the house, for the chimneys had been smoking. The grass on the lawn was lashed into white streaks by the wind before which the hens ran sideways, like old ladies crossing the road. There was a thick scum at one side of the broad ditch, a scum of withered catkins fallen from the black poplars. Catkins hung like funereal trappings or like black caterpillars on every twig of the apple trees; on the ditch, the ducks were dancing on the waves.

"Such a wind as this scatters the seeds," said Anne. "The winged fruits of the elms and the maples are whirled up from the ditches where they have been lying all the winter, and are carried over the tops of the tallest trees, and this wind will gather me up like a seed that has lain too long under the tree from which it fell. Heaven knows where it will carry me! To Egypt or Greece, maybe, or perhaps only to pull the rug over the knees of an old lady driving her donkey-cart along the lanes of an adjoining parish."

Under the avenue of elms the wind roared so loud that Anne feared for the safety of the trees, and stepped cautiously, looking up among the swaying branches. In her hand she held the precious letter that was to set her free, the letter which was to her as the wing is to the seed.

" Once this is posted, there is no turning back," she thought. " There will be difficulties, but they will be overcome, and when I look back on my life I shall say it began on the day when I posted this letter, and I shall remember the March gale roaring like a lion among the elms."

A vision of an elderly lady with soft brown eyes like bees, and short grey hair, haunted her: a precise lady she would be, perhaps one who had been an actress or an opera singer in her day, and kept a casket of love-letters from all the poets of the 'eighties standing on the table beside her. Her employer would laugh gently at her enthusiasm, and would tell her wonderful anecdotes. Her name would be beautiful, and familiar: a name that is to be found in every catalogue of roses, for she was the kind of lady after whom roses are named. Anne would take the place of a daughter, and would soon inherit all her passionate fire tempered by her knowledge of the world, all her deep wisdom born of experience and of renunciation; all her cynical clear-sighted witty tenderness. . . .

"Good morning, Miss Dunnock." Anne's day-dream was interrupted, and she looked down to find Rachel Sotheby standing before her, her bright eyes shining, and her cheeks flushed by the wind. Anne was pleased to see the little girl, and thinking that they must part soon, she bent down to kiss her, a thing she had not done before. As she did so, she remembered Mr. Yockney's remark about Rachel's boots and glanced at them. Yes, they were stiff little boots, cracked behind the toe-caps, worn out, they would let in the water.

"Mr. Yockney was quite right," she said to herself, and entering the post office, was embarrassed to find a stranger standing at the counter writing a telegram.

"This must be Rachel's brother," she

thought as she recognized the foxey nose,
and the slit eyes of the photograph she
had seen in the grocer's parlour. " This
must be Richard Sotheby, who has been
turned into a gentleman while his little
sister has holes in her boots."

As Anne asked for her postal order she
avoided looking at the young man of
whom she had heard so much, but while
she was waiting for the pen (there was
only one in the post office with which it
was possible to write) she could not keep
her eyes turned away, and when he had
finished his telegram, she had to meet his
eye as he handed her the pen. The action
was polite, but though their eyes met for
an instant, she could see that it was mechan-
ical, she had not engaged his attention,
he was thinking of his telegram, and next
moment she heard him spelling it over to
Mrs. Day, the post-mistress, and explaining that it was in French.

" *The Church Times* . . ." wrote Anne.

" G...R...A...N...D...I...S...O...N," spelt
the young man.

" Barclays Bank and Co.," wrote Anne,
keeping her ears open but failing to follow
the address.

She had filled in her postal order and

had sealed up her letter; there was no reason to stay longer listening while Mrs. Day repeated the letters after him, and she went out, posted her letter, and turned homewards. Already her emotions about her advertisement had subsided, and as she hurried under the storm-tossed elms her thoughts were occupied with the grocer's son and his strange telegram.

" Je suis las de tes amourettes et de mon amour. Je consens. Ecris." What did that mean? And who was the Grandison to whom it was addressed?

Her meditations were interrupted by Richard Sotheby himself, who passed her, walking rapidly down the avenue. His hat was jammed hard on his head: he did not lift it, and directly he had passed she noticed that he was wearing button boots made of patent leather.

Chapter 7

THE BURNT FARM

THE March gale continued for several days; the daffodils were broken, the hyacinths in the border laid low, but one morning Anne awoke to find that not a breath of wind was stirring in the elms, and after an hour or so the sun was blazing with the heat of June. On the breakfast table lay *The Church Times*, and she trembled with emotion when she saw it in her father's hands.

" I must speak to him," she said to herself, " I must speak to him now," but she did not speak, consoling herself for her lack of resolution with the thought that the earliest answers to her advertisement could not arrive for two days since they were to be forwarded from the office in Fleet Street; she had not given her name and address, but had used a box number.

" I will speak to him to-morrow," she said to herself. " For I would like to enjoy one day of perfect spring weather before I leave Dry Coulter, and our conversation is certain to upset us."

She waited eagerly until the birds' breakfast left her free to take the newspaper into her hands. Her advertisement was in, and reading the modest three lines Anne felt her heart swell with the triumph of authorship, and she ran upstairs with *The Church Times* in her hand to read the announcement over and over to herself in private.

" There is no turning back now! " she exclaimed. " I have shown my independence; I have taken the first step, and nothing now can keep me from achieving my purpose."

Anne's eyes flashed as she turned to the looking-glass; and the eager look she met there intoxicated her; at that moment she almost suffocated with the sense of her own power. The blood rushed to her head, and she clenched her fists, and ground her teeth in the effort to remain calm.

" Have you seen *The Church Times*? " called Mr. Dunnock, coming back from watching the birds.

" Here it is, father," she answered, and running downstairs surrendered it to him without a tremor. Her father took it absentmindedly, saying as he did so:

" I think there is some straw somewhere, my dear. Would you ask Noah to scatter it about the lawn? It will be useful for the sparrows; the nearest rick is several hundred yards away, a long journey for them, almost an impossible one if the wind should veer to the east. On a calm day like this, it is not so important, but there are not many calm days in March, and in any case it will save a great deal of trouble."

At another moment Anne might have been vexed at her father's solicitude for the hated sparrows, but she was in a mood to forgive him his follies, and she ran off at once to the potting-shed to find the straw, and scattered it on the lawn herself.

All the morning she was beside herself with excitement; and she found it hard to answer Maggie sensibly when she spoke of their plan of whitewashing the scullery. When the proposal had been put forward a fortnight before by Anne, it had seemed to mark an epoch, but Maggie found that it was suddenly brushed on one side, her feelings were hurt, the date was left uncertain, and Anne had fled out into the garden before she had time to question her again.

The first tulips were standing stiffly to attention in their field-grey uniforms, their buds unopened, but the girl could not think of tulips as she paced up and down the borders. Her life at the vicarage was coming to an end, and she must speak to her father, but after thinking over what she would say for an hour, she could find no words, and came to the conclusion that it would be unwise to open the subject before she had decided where she was going. Her father would be certain to raise objections, and they would appear more formidable if her plans were not fixed. It would be better for both of them if the parting were to come suddenly.

"I will go to him in his study," she said. "When my bag is packed," and with this settled in her mind she felt happy for the first time that morning. She had come out to enjoy the warm spring weather, but, as soon as she had decided not to speak to her father, and before she had time to look about her, she saw Maggie waving from the kitchen door and knew that it was time for lunch.

After the strain of making plans about her future she found the meal a pleasant one, emotion had given her an appetite, and, as she ate, Anne enjoyed listening to her father inveighing against the stupidity of old Noah.

" You would scarcely believe it," said Mr. Dunnock, " but within half an hour of your having scattered the straw, that old fool was sweeping it up. I ordered him to stop, but he would not listen to me until I had taken him by the arm and had explained my reasons. But so blind is the prejudice of the rustics about here, that he said that he would as soon poison the sparrows as not. I was forced to speak to him very severely. It is his first lapse since the question of the strawberry nets last year."

The mild sunlit air was full of bees as Anne left the vicarage after lunch; the celandines were gaping in the sunlight on the bank above the Broad Ditch. Wagtails ran round the water's edge, goldfinches flew up into the elms, and yellowhammers trotted before her on the road.

As she passed the Post Office she remembered Richard Sotheby and his strange telegram, and tired of the turmoil of her own emotion, she welcomed the memory. " I am tired of thy little love affairs and of my own love. I consent. Write." And pondering over these words she asked herself what kind of creature the Grandison might be to whom they were addressed.

A rich woman in Paris, it seemed reasonable to suppose, who had been his mistress. . . . . "It is to secure her love that little Rachel is neglected." Anne wondered what their life had been in Paris, and slowly a picture of Miss Grandison formed itself clearly in her mind— a fair woman she must be, with a white skin like the flesh of a hazel nut, with fair, almost colourless hair and light blue eyes, a thick, slightly aquiline nose. . . . That certainly was Miss Grandison, and at the opera she wore diamonds and was wrapped in white fur. On summer evenings her habit must be to drive with Sotheby out of Paris in her limousine to have supper in the open air of lobsters and cream, raspberries and iced champagne. . . . As the night drew on she would become bored, and drag young Sotheby after her to a vast hotel in Paris where they could dance all night. The men in their starched shirtfronts would turn pale, and wilt in the small hours of the morning under the tropical palms, but La Grandison would dance on and on, ruthlessly, first with one man and then with another. Richard Sotheby would be forgotten, a young man from the Peruvian Embassy would escort her home, while Richard, disconsolate and broken-hearted, would be left to pay for the buckets of iced champagne, and the mounds of uneaten sandwiches. . . . No wonder, with such a woman, that he should declare he was weary of her love affairs and of his love. But there was a hint of jealousy in his bitterness.

Anne smiled contentedly. Richard Sotheby's telegram enabled her to see her own life with more philosophy. Soon she forgot to think, and walked slowly onwards, happy in feeling the soft air caress her cheek, in hearing the chatter of starlings in the orchard trees, in looking about her in idleness. Ewes lay indolently on the green, their lambs were already strong on their legs, and she watched the play of the pair nearest to her, at one moment butting each other; in the next skipping behind each other, or mounting on one another in amorous curvets and then suddenly indifferent, breaking off their play.

The stream was still swollen, though rain had not fallen for a week. Anne crossed it by the little bridge beside the water splash, and made her way across the green, the sheep scattering as she passed. On each side of the old track that led to the burnt farmhouse, the black-thorn bushes were in flower. The masses of frail blossom were full of the humming of bees, but as yet there were no wild flowers in the hedge, only an occasional celandine shone on the bank like a dropped sovereign.

The fields on each side were hired by a farmer living at a distance; they were still cultivated and kept in some sort of repair, but much had gone to ruin since the farm-house had been burnt. The hedges had not been cut for years; there were forest trees in them, and holes big enough for bullocks to wander through. The great stretch of pasture by the farm itself, the home meadows where the prize herd of spotted cows used to be milked in the open, that had gone out of cultivation, and was full of hawthorn bushes, of the trailing briars of dog-roses and of brambles. The finest pasture which had yielded the richest butter was become no more than a covert where the French partridges nested. Of the farmhouse itself there was nothing left but a few of the walls, heaps of plaster where the nettles grew in summer, and one or two blackened beams. The vegetable garden was a wilderness with a quarter of an acre of horseradish and matted gooseberry bushes buried in convolvulus. At one side, on a smooth expanse of turf, stood the old square dove house, as sound as the day it had been built, and the pigeons came and went as they had always done, for the dove house was still used as a granary, and the pigeons were the perquisite of a farm-hand.

As Anne came in front of the house, it seemed strange to her to see the fine iron gates, with great ilexes on either side of them, and the flagged path that ran so cleanly up to a mere heap of broken bricks, where the front door had been. Not a weed had taken root on the pathway, not a bramble strayed across it, and even the pond, by whose bricked side it ran, was clear water. Irises grew there and flowered in the summer time; on the grassy bank opposite there were daffodils in bloom. Anne let herself in at the iron gates, thinking to herself that it was very strange that no farmhouse had been rebuilt there on the site of the old one, that no labourer had been allowed to work the rich garden as his allotment, and that it was impossible to guess why everything should have been let go to ruin except the square dove house of red brick, which must have stood for three centuries and which looked as if it would stand for as many more. All about there were the traces of a former fruitfulness, a great walnut overshadowed one of the ancient yards by the edge of the pond, and on the other side, hidden in an impenetrable thicket of bullaces, giant pear trees and plum suckers, laced about with bramble and dog-rose, was the orchard. The plums were bursting into a fine blow, and Anne wondered whether the boys came there to rob the fruit, or whether the plums and apples fell of their own weight, or hung until the wasps had hollowed out the last of them. She wondered how it was that she had never met anyone by the burnt farm, never a child nor a village labourer. She had not seen it before in spring, though in the summer it had been a favourite haunt of hers; and she had gathered roses there late on into the autumn from a bush which had not yet gone wild. As she walked up the path she smelt a breath of wood smoke, and turning the corner of the house by what had been the chimney stack, she saw tongues of flame shooting up, and heard the crackle of sticks. "A tramp, or perhaps an encampment of gypsies," she said to herself, and would have drawn back, but at that instant she caught sight of Rachel Sotheby coming from the orchard with an armful of dry sticks.

"Why, Rachel, are you having a picnic here?" she asked, seeing a kettle on the fire.

Rachel came running to her with eyes that shone with excitement; she had lost her grave look of self-possession, so that it was natural for Anne to stoop to kiss her for the second time, seduced by her wild look and her tangled curls.

"Yes, Miss Dunnock. Do you come here often? I have never been here before, but my brother brought me. He is sketching the house from the other side."

Anne would have taken her leave on hearing of Richard Sotheby's presence, but Rachel would not let her go before she had gathered her some daffodils from the far side of the pond, and had shown her the white violets growing under the

107

walnut tree. The kettle had not boiled when they came back to the fire, and as Richard Sotheby was nowhere to be seen, she sat down for a little while, talking to the little girl while she heaped up the sticks and unpacked the basket. A minute passed when suddenly she heard a step, and, jumping up, saw that Richard Sotheby was standing a yard or two behind her. He was bare-headed, frowning, his lips twitching, and seeing Anne at the same moment as she saw him, he gave his sister rather a puzzled glance.

" This is my brother Richard," said Rachel, looking up from blowing the fire. " Richard, this is Miss Dunnock."

The young man's face broke into smiles at her name, and he held out his hand.

" I am very pleased to meet you," said Anne, taking it. " Now I must be getting on. Good-bye, Rachel."

" Please don't go," said the grocer's son. " I have finished work for to-day; the light has changed, and I have been wanting to meet you. I want to ask you all about how your doorstep was ploughed up. I shall never meet anyone else to whom such a thing has happened, and I want to know what it felt like."

Anne was too much taken aback by this to know what to answer, but just at that moment they were interrupted by Rachel's saying that the tea was made.

Young Sotheby repeated his invitation, and Anne sat down on a block of stone which had once supported the corner of a haystack, feeling very foolish, shy, and ashamed of her shyness, but she was determined that she would not run away after what he had said. She had blushed crimson when he had spoken of Plough Monday, but it had pleased her to hear something spoken of openly about which so much must have been said behind her back.

" Yes. Our doorstep was ploughed up," she said, and her voice sounded to the others as though she were angry. " Why does it interest you? "

" It was very wicked of the men to do it," said Rachel suddenly. " And you ought not to speak of such a thing to Miss Dunnock, Richard."

The grocer's son laughed at his sister's indignant interruption. " Rachel is a great friend of yours, Miss Dunnock. I shall have to apologise to her, but I hope I have not offended you also."

" No. Not at all. I want to talk about it, Rachel," she said, looking at the child. The little girl's mouth was trembling.

" That don't matter," she said, almost crying. " Richard did not ought to have spoken to you of that thing. Mother told everyone that what they done was no better than if they were heathens, and that no one was to say a word about it. No one would have ever but our Richard."

Anne took Rachel on to her knees, and hugged the child close; at that moment she was near to tears herself, for the first time in her life she understood that she had neighbours who loved her, and did not think of her only as a queer girl, and the daughter of a queer clergyman.

" Sit here, close to me," she said, letting the child go. " And let me talk to your brother because he is very clever and is . . ." It was on the tip of her tongue to say " a gentleman," but she altered it to: " because I am sure he would never be unkind."

Rachel looked at him in a way which threatened that if he were unkind to Miss Dunnock there would be terrible consequences, and Richard Sotheby poured out the tea in silence, until Anne asked him again why he was interested in the ploughing up of the doorstep.

"Because it was, as my mother said, a heathenish act, and I imagine that, like most heathen things, it must have been beautiful."

"Yes, it was beautiful," replied Anne instantly. "It was so beautiful that I was fascinated watching it, and though I was crying with shame, I was glad that they had done it."

Richard Sotheby grinned with interest as Anne said this, and nodded his head several times.

"Like a rape," he said under his breath. His words were not meant for Anne to hear, but she had caught the word, and for some minutes did not know what to say or where to look, but sat praying with all her soul that she would not blush. At last the danger passed, and she went on to speak of the plough wobbling a little as it ran through the earth, and of the broad, shiny backs of the three chestnut horses, and the handsome face opposite her quickened with pleasure as she told how it happened after a fall of snow, and that there was snow on the horses' manes and on the carters' caps.

When she had described the whole scene, he pressed her for further details, and soon she found that she was speaking of her feelings after the event, and that he was listening in silence. She pulled herself up suddenly, unwilling to tell him so much about herself, and there was a long silence, for the young man did not press her with questions, but the silence was broken at last by Anne saying: "But you cannot understand it unless I were to tell you about my father."

"Of course it came about through him in the first place," said Richard Sotheby reflectively, and Anne would have begun to speak of her father and her feelings for him if she had not felt Rachel shiver, and then she perceived that the sun was sinking low, and that it had grown cold for sitting out of doors.

"That is too long a story," she said, rising to her feet. "You would not understand it, and if you did, it would bore you. But it is late now, and I must be going home."

"You must promise to tell me another time," said the grocer's son. "If the weather keeps fine I shall be working here every afternoon, until about half-past three when the light changes. Come and have tea with me to-morrow and finish your story."

Anne promised to come, and then gathering up her flowers and saying good-bye to Rachel, she hurried off, for young Sotheby had to go back to his easel and put it away in the dove house, and she had no wish to be seen walking home with him.

Chapter 8

WILLOW-PATTERN PARIS

FOR several days a gentle wind blew from the west and the cloudiness of dew-drenched mornings was followed by the sunshine and softness of the afternoons. Anne Dunnock knew that the grocer's son was painting at the Burnt Farm, but though each day she set out in that direction, she always turned aside on the way, breaking her promise that she would meet him there again.

" I spoke to him too freely; Heaven knows what he must think of me! " she repeated to herself. At moments she found it consoling to remember that she felt quite sure that she did not like Richard Sotheby, but at other times it seemed to her that what was so terrible was to have confided so much of her secret life to a man whom she disliked. But the weather was too beautiful for her to remain long unhappy for such reasons, and nearly her whole day was spent out of doors. In the morning she would busy herself in the garden, and, tempted by the sunshine, Mr. Dunnock would leave his study to come and stand beside her while she sowed the sweet peas and the mignonette, or planted out young wallflowers in the borders.

" Do not forget to sow teazles by the pond," he would remind her. " They are as handsome as hollyhocks, and wherever there have been teazles in summer time the goldfinches will come in winter."

Anne did not regard the teazle as a weed, she loved the plant's bold leaves that hold hands about the prickly stem, making a cup to catch the rain, and the flower-heads with their bands of blue which creep up and down the inflorescence.

Few words passed between father and daughter, yet both were happy as they went together to sow the teazle seed that he had saved, and were conscious of being in sympathy with one another as they had scarcely been all the winter. Once there was a rose tree to be transplanted; on another occasion a rambler which had been blown down had to be nailed up on the far side of the summer-house, and while Anne shovelled the earth round the roots, and drove the nails through strips cut from an old stair carpet, Mr. Dunnock held the tree upright and the creeper in place, his hands protected in Noah's hedging gloves.

" The bees are working in the willows," he said. " Though it is still three weeks to Palm Sunday."

Yet Anne had not abandoned her plan; it was only that the spring and the garden full of growing things had claimed her attention. But one morning she found a letter for her on the breakfast table, and as she opened it her heart sank, for she guessed that it was from a lady anxious to engage her as a companion.

" What am I to say to him? " she asked herself, looking up at her father as he came into the room, and the morning was spent wandering about the house, first carrying an old trunk out of the boxroom to pack her things, and then with pale cheeks running to the door of her father's study. She did not knock, when she stood trembling outside the door, though she knew that in a day or two at most, per-haps even in a few hours, she would be leaving the vicarage.

During luncheon she came nearest to speaking to her father, but each time, just as she was going to begin, she was interrupted by some remark of his. Such a subject could not be opened without perparation, when her father spoke of the decoration of the church at Easter her courage failed her, and before she had recovered it, he had shaken the crumbs off his waistcoat and had gone into his study.

"I shall have to leave a letter for him to read after I am gone," said Anne, but the idea was hateful to her; it revealed her own cowardice too clearly, and when she began to compose the letter that should be left behind, she found the task an impossible one.

"A walk will help me to think things out," but in the road her footsteps turned of themselves across the green, and she was half-way to the burnt farm before she stopped suddenly, realising that she was going there to lay her difficulties before the grocer's son.

"That will be the best way," she said aloud. "In such a position as mine, one must seek advice, for it is only when one has been advised by someone else that one recovers confidence in the sanity of one's own opinions."

Directly she had passed through the

iron gates the sunshine seemed warmer; it was as hot as June; she could see the daffodils clustering on the banks of the pond and reflected in its waters; a brimstone butterfly rose from the flagged pathway and rambled in front of her, settling at last on one of the brick walls.

There was a continuous cooing from the top of the dove house, and the beat of the wings of the pigeons coming and going; a blackbird was singing in the tangled orchard.

Rachel Sotheby was nowhere to be seen; there was no fire burning, but recollecting that Richard Sotheby would be painting on the other side of the house, Anne walked round into the wild garden. She could not see him, and soon sat down, putting her arms up to tidy her hair, loosened by an angry toss of her head, for she was vexed to have come looking for the young man.

"Please stay like that," said a sharp voice behind her, and she looked round to find Richard Sotheby watching her from inside the ruined walls.

"Please stay where you are, Miss Dunnock," he repeated. "You are exactly what I want in my picture; I knew there

was something needed;—now I see that
it is a figure."

But Anne jumped up before the sentence was finished, and Richard Sotheby
climbed out of the ruin with his palate in
his hand and a frown on his face, repeating, " Please stay there. . . ."

He was insistent, and Anne had to agree
to sit for a few minutes while he made a
charcoal drawing.

" When I have finished you shall have
tea," he said as though he were speaking
to a child. Anne sat, looking up at the sky
with her hands to her hair and her elbows
up, as he had posed her, saying to herself
that she had never met anyone with such
bad manners.

She was hot with annoyance, but soon
the blush left her cheek, and while she
listened to the pigeons her resentment
faded away.

" May I see your picture? " she asked
five minutes later, and when the artist
refused, shaking his head and laughing,
she felt no irritation. It seemed natural to
her that he should say: " Not till it is
finished."

" When will that be? " she asked remembering her own departure.

"It will take me a week to put in that figure; I don't know how I shall do it unless you sit for me. Come, let us have tea."

"I am afraid I cannot sit, Mr. Sotheby," said Anne. "I have come to-day to say good-bye."

The young man opened his eyes at this; his curiosity had to be satisfied, and soon Anne was telling him that her life was being wasted at the vicarage, and that she was determined to leave her father.

Richard Sotheby listened without saying a word; he was kneeling in front of the little fire he had just lighted. The sticks smouldered but went out when the paper had burnt away, and she paused in her story while he fetched a bottle of turpentine from his paint-box. He sprinkled a little of the spirit, and a thick yellow flame sprang up; then the sticks crackled. All his attention seemed to be for the fire, only when she spoke of the advertisement he turned his head sharply to look at her, and when she told him that an answer had come that morning he exclaimed: "Extraordinary!" under his breath.

"But what does your father say to all this?" he asked suddenly, as he handed her the cup of tea he had poured out. Anne found the confession of her cowardice was difficult; Sotheby was staring at her as if he were surprised by her words.

" I think that would be behaving very heartlessly," he said when she had done. He filled the lid of the kettle with tea, blew on it and added: " It would be a great shock to him, and it seems to me so unnecessary. Children have parents so much at their mercy; their one duty to them, surely, is to avoid shattering their illusions. I'm not a good son; my father is excessively irritating; quite as irritating as yours. I don't love him, and that makes me feel ashamed. . . . You have left it so late. . . . Do you really think that getting this place is worth having to behave so badly? "

Anne's face fell, and rather sulkily she pulled the letter she had got that morning out of her pocket.

Richard Sotheby glanced at it, wrinkled his nose, and began reading it aloud:

"Spion Kop,"
14A Kimberley Road,
West Sutton Vallance,
London, W.23.

Dear Madam,

I have seen your advertisement in *The Church Times*, and think it possible that you may suit me. I am looking for a companion of gentle birth who would be willing to undertake light duties in the house. I have a girl who comes in daily. What I really require is someone who will, as far as possible, take the place of my own devoted and dearly-loved daughter who died last year after a long illness, patiently borne.

I would introduce you to a pleasant circle of friends, and would look after you as I think you will agree, a girl should be looked after on coming so near London. I cannot offer a high wage, but you will have every home comfort. Will you please tell me in your answer, your age, and whether you have been away from home before, and when you can come up for me to interview you. It is essential that you should be fond of dogs, but no doubt you are. This neighbourhood is considered a very healthy one, and the house is next door to the church.

Yours faithfully,
ETHEL CROWLINK.

Each phrase had sounded comic as he read it aloud, and his voice ended with such a queer note that Anne burst out laughing.

" You think I oughtn't to go to her? " she said.

" It is ridiculous to think of it," he answered. " Not for your father's sake but for your own. It would be out of the frying-pan into the fire: surely you see that? "

She did not answer, and he went on: " Why should you choose to live with the horrid old woman who wrote this letter, in a London suburb? If you must leave home. . . ."

" I must . . ." she said. " Better anything, however horrid it may sound. If I do not get away from home, I shall never be able to speak to anyone."

There was a long silence while she watched Richard Sotheby wrinkling up his nose.

" You may be more unhappy when

you can speak, Anne. Particularly if you should fall in love. That makes one more unhappy than anything else. However, you would do better to go as an English governess in a French family. In that way you would see new people and have quite fresh experiences."

And Richard Sotheby began to speak of Paris, while Anne sat fascinated by the magic flow of words, seeing pictures of a great town full of avenues and open spaces, with a twisting river, crossed by innumerable bridges. And for some reason, though she knew that Paris was a huge city, and though Richard spoke often of the crowds thronging the boulevards, she imagined Paris as a willow-pattern plate; its bridges like that steep bridge over which a blue figure is hurrying, with bald-headed Chinamen fishing in the winding river beside it on which a barge is floating, a lady is disembarking, and weeping willow trees border the Elysian fields.

The voice went on, and Anne watching the fine forehead and the abstracted eyes, gazing into the fire, was carried away by her imagination and saw herself living in the willow-pattern city.

"That will be wonderful," she said.

"But what am I to say in my letter to Mrs. Crowlink?"

She spoke in a tone of such despair that he burst out laughing at her. "You are a child!" he said, but his voice was too pleasant for her to take offence, and for the first time she knew the sweetness of being laughed at without minding it. "I feel sure of his sympathy," she said to herself. "Though I came here believing that I disliked him, and even now I am not sure what I think of him."

Richard Sotheby had gathered his brushes together, and was pouring water from the kettle on to the ashes.

"You will come and sit to me to-morrow, won't you?" he asked. "And then we can go on with our discussion of your future. Come at half-past two, but now we had better go home separately, otherwise we shall see our names written up on Lambert's Barn: 'Richard Sotheby loves Anne Dunnock and takes her to the Burnt Farm.' I wonder if they would put 'the dirty dog,' or 'bless his heart,' after my name? It is usually one or the other."

Anne laughed at this, and looked the grocer's son in the eyes, but his glance was one of mere amusement.

"Oh, they would put 'the dirty dog' after your name" she said suddenly.

"You are quite right," he said laughing. "Wonderful you should guess." He did not offer to shake hands, and she walked away.

She had read the scrawls chronicling the loves of the village boys and girls, but she had never thought that it would be possible to speak of them. As she hurried home her heart was beating fast; she looked neither to left nor right, but kept repeating to herself: "Richard Sotheby loves Anne Dunnock, the dirty dog!" "But he doesn't," she added, wondering if she would wish to be loved by him.

Then she repeated as a variation: "Richard Sotheby doesn't love Anne Dunnock, the dirty dog!" That was more like the truth! And she thought of the telegram she had seen him write, and wondered if he would tell her about La Grandison. Perhaps one day soon she would see her, alighting from a barge in the Seine that ran through a willow-pattern Paris.

There were no other answers to her advertisement, and as soon as the lying letter to Mrs. Crowlink had been posted,

Anne was free to forget her problems. The week which followed passed happily enough; every afternoon she sat for an hour or more in the spring sunlight talking to Richard Sotheby while he painted her, answering his questions about her childhood at Ely, describing the poverty in which they had lived, and how her mother had been looked down upon by the ladies of the cathedral set, then telling him of her father's eccentricities, and his violent temper, and of the last outburst when he had insulted a canon, and had been sent for by the Bishop, and of how he had been kept to lunch at the palace and sent away with the words: " I think you will do better by yourself, Mr. Dunnock. There is a living going begging at Dry Coulter. A hundred and twenty pounds a year. . . ."

The pigeons cooed through all the afternoon, the pear tree burst into flower over her head, and was filled with the hum of hundreds of bees working among the scarlet stamens, at intervals Anne spoke of her life, and every now and then Richard would interrupt her with questions about her father. When she told of his love for the birds, Richard was delighted, and the rest of the afternoon was spent describing all his little acts of tenderness and consideration: scattering straw for the sparrows to build their nests, sowing teazles for the goldfinches. . .

" I see that I should get on much better with your father than you do," he said. " We should have a great deal in common."

" He has made me hate birds," said Anne. " Sometimes I think I should like to wear a bird in my hat."

" You feel about birds what I feel about love and about religion, I suppose," said Richard.

" My father has got birds and religion all mixed up, somehow," said Anne, but when he asked her to explain, all she could say was: " I don't understand it, and I can't explain it, but I know I am right. It is difficult to tell often of which he is speaking."

" That seems rather a beautiful confusion to me," said Richard. " Just listen for a moment to the pigeons in the dove house and you will feel inclined to it yourself."

" I only hate them because I am wicked and selfish," said Anne. " I am not going

128

to sacrifice all my life to beautiful things. Father can only see beauty in a chaffinch or a wagtail; I might be beautiful too, but he would never notice it."

Richard laughed at this outburst. " As pretty as a wagtail," he mused, screwing up his eyes, and teasing her. " That is flying rather high, isn't it? "

" I don't see why a human being shouldn't be as beautiful as a bird," said Anne seriously, at which her companion laughed more than ever.

" Perhaps not," he said. " Still you don't really hope that anyone should ever say to you: ' Miss Dunnock, you are as pretty as a hedge-sparrow.' I, of course, with my long nose, am rather like a snipe." Then, changing his tone, he went on: " You are more like a heron than a hedge-sparrow: a tall ghostly figure seen by moonlight standing in the reeds at the water's edge. The heron's hair is always flying loose like yours; he tries in vain to keep it up with fish bones."

" I am going to cut all my hair off! " cried Anne savagely.

" Yes, I think you would look better," said Richard simply. " But you must not do that until my picture is finished.

Seriously, if you want admiration, you should come to Paris. You are quite sure to find someone there who will think you are beautiful."

She bit her lip, and asked herself if Richard could have told her more plainly, to her face, that he did not think so.

" He does not care for me," she said to herself as she walked home the following afternoon, after the last sitting. " Had he cared for me, he would have said something nice to me when he said good-bye. He is only amused, and contemptuous. Thank Heaven I did not show him any of my drawings! "

For she had taken out her drawing book that morning, to try her hand at fashion plates, and had sat a long while examining her old careful sketches of a dead-nettle in flower and a spray of honey-suckle in bud, only to put them away at last guessing that her work would not make Richard Sotheby take her any more seriously, though an ambition to earn her living by drawing clothes was still present in her mind.

" Yet he likes me, I am sure of that," she said. " He would not teaze me otherwise." The thought consoled her, and she crossed the green more happily. Suddenly she heard a little cry behind her, a sharp note like the clink of flint on steel, and looking round she saw Rachel.

"Will you come to tea to-morrow?" the child asked when she had overtaken her. "It is my birthday and mother told me I might ask anyone that I liked."

Chapter 9

BIRTHDAY TEA

ANNE sat down to tea on the following afternoon, with the four Sothebys, round an iced cake with thirteen candles, in the rather dark little room where she had retired to hide her tears after Plough Monday, darker now, for it was raining outside. There were chocolate biscuits in glass dishes and crackers lying on the table between the plates. But in spite of the air of jollity, and of Rachel's excitement, Anne felt just as she had done on the first occasion she had entered the room: anxious to escape.

Rachel had met her at the door, they had kissed, and she had given the little girl a pair of fur-lined slippers as a birthday present, but immediately afterwards Mrs. Sotheby had begun to introduce her to Richard and he had no sooner cut his mother short by saying that they were acquainted already, when the grocer came up and said: " Miss Dunnock, this is my son Richard of whom I think I have spoken to you. . . ."

" Miss Dunnock and I have met," said

Richard, and Anne added: " Richard and
I are old friends already," but at once
became aware that what she said was the
wrong thing, for there was an expression
of astonishment, almost of alarm, possibly
even of disapproval, on Mr. Sotheby's
face. Certainly he seemed nervous as he
said: " Well, well, since I find we are all
acquainted let us sit down to tea."

The difficulties of the introduction were
forgotten in the excitement of cutting the
cake, and it was not long before the last
of the crackers was pulled; a yellow paper
crown was found for Mr. Sotheby; there
were paper caps for the rest of the company, and though several of the mottoes
alluded to Christmas, they were read aloud
with pleasure and received with delight.

" It is too bad, Richard," said Mr.
Sotheby over his third cup of tea. " You
are going away the day after to-morrow,
and you have never painted the portrait
of your mother, for which I have asked
so often."

Anne felt numb on hearing that Richard
was going away in two days' time: "Why
didn't he tell me that? " she asked herself,
but without noticing her look the grocer
went on: " You have spent all your time

out sketching the old Manor House, but you have not shown us any of your work."

"He brought it back to-day," said Mrs. Sotheby. "But I haven't seen it." Richard was reluctant to show his picture, but at last he left the room, and it was only then, seeing Rachel was trembling, and upset about something, that Anne suddenly remembered that the Sothebys might easily recognise the figure of the girl in the foreground, engaged in doing up her hair.

Richard lifted an eyebrow at her as he put the canvas on the mantel-piece, and there was a long silence, a silence which grew alarming, and Anne knew that she had been recognised.

"This figure is you, Miss Dunnock," said the grocer at last, speaking stiffly.

"Miss Dunnock came by while I was making tea for Richard," said Rachel in her precise tone, and everyone in the room breathed more freely. "She stayed to tea with us."

"And she was good enough to pose for me while I drew a sketch of her to put into the foreground," said Richard.

"It was very kind of you to be sure," said his father.

" I think you ought to be ashamed of yourself, Richard," said Mrs. Sotheby. " Putting Miss Dunnock into your horrid picture like that; you haven't done her justice at all. I should scarcely have recognised her." And the grocer's wife gave Anne a little smile to tell her that she did not mind Richard's having painted her instead of the portrait that his father wanted.

" I should never have sat to him," said Anne. " If I had known that he ought to have been painting your portrait," but Mr. Sotheby was saying that he had to be off on business.

" Very, very kind of you to come on Rachel's birthday," he said as he left the room.

" No, indeed, there is hardly any resemblance at all," said Mrs. Sotheby. " Anyone might think it was one of the Puttys come home again."

" Who are the Puttys? " asked Anne.

" What, you don't mean to say that you have never heard of the Putty's! " exclaimed Rachel and her mother together, and Richard, who had been looking glum since he had shown his picture, added: " Yes, you ought to hear that

135

story since you are the only other person that has turned the ploughmen away."

"How can you say such a thing, Richard!" said Mrs. Sotheby. "You know how that came about by a mistake," but Anne asked:

"Did the Putty's have their doorstep ploughed up?"

"No, not the Putty's," was the answer, and as Anne seemed mystified but eager to hear more Richard said: "Come mother, tell Miss Dunnock the whole story from the beginning." And Rachel also added her request for the story.

"Well, wait a moment till I have cleared away the tea-things," said Mrs. Sotheby, work that was soon done with both Rachel and Anne helping. While they were out of the room Richard seized the opportunity to take his canvas off the mantelpiece. He hid it in the woodshed and came back feeling happier.

The chairs were drawn up round the fire, Rachel sitting at Anne's knee and holding her hand, and Mrs. Sotheby began:

"What you children call the 'Burnt Farm' is really the ruins of a manor house; the squire lived there, Captain Purdue, and since the burning there has been no squire at Dry Coulter. I can remember him very well: a tall man who had been a captain in the navy, and he certainly thought a great deal about appearances. One could tell that just by looking at him; what one could not have told was that he cared a great deal about money too."

" You have forgotten to say that he had been dismissed the service," Richard reminded his mother.

" Well, his ship was wrecked, you know, and he left the navy after that; I have heard that he was turned out because of it, but I do not really know," said Mrs. Sotheby. " Certainly he was a very unlucky man, but at first all went well; he had a fine house, built in the time of King Charles II (Oliver's men had burnt the old house down in the civil wars), and a wonderful garden (he had a whole greenhouse full of arum lilies in the winter), his horses were famous, and his dairy cows won prizes. At that time there was not a gentleman's place for miles round that was kept up better. But I should have said that Captain Purdue was married, to a very good-looking lady indeed. She was a good deal younger than he was, and I think she came from the Channel Islands. But they had no children."

There was the jangle of the shop bell. Mrs. Sotheby broke off her sentence and started to her feet, but Rachel had slipped out into the shop before her, and they could hear a woman saying that she had just run across for a bar of soap, and then, when she had made her purchase, ask: " It is your birthday, isn't it, Rachel? Many happy returns! How does it feel to be grown up? " and the little girl answer: " Very pleasant indeed, thank you very much, Mrs. Papworth."

" The first of the Captain's misfortunes," continued Mrs. Sotheby, " was that his wife ran away from him, and it was not long after that before he was killed in an accident. He was having his barn altered; it was an old building, nearly as old as the house, and he wanted to make it a couple of feet higher and was having the roof raised on jacks. They got one side of it up some inches, and then the foreman sent for him to tell him that it couldn't be done. The Captain went to see for himself but he would not listen to anything the men said, but gave the word to go on with the work, and they

had not given the screws on the other side
half a dozen turns before the main beam
broke in two and the whole roof fell in
on them. Captain Purdue was standing
just underneath, and was killed, and three
of the men were badly injured. You see
it was no one's fault but his own, and
indeed it was very lucky that others were
not killed beside himself."

"But how did the house get burnt,
and what had the ploughmen to do with
it?" asked Anne.

"Nothing at all," answered Mrs. Sotheby with a laugh. "But some of the most
ignorant of the men said that his bad luck
was because they had ploughed the doorstep up. That's why it was so wrong of
them to behave like that to your father if
they really believe what they say. But I
don't think they do believe such things
nowadays: everyone laughs at them, but
I think people will do anything if it is the
custom."

"So they are expecting us to have
bad luck?" asked Anne with her face
suddenly serious.

Richard looked at her rather maliciously
and laughed.

"Yes, we all expect you to run away

from home and your father to fall out of a tree and break his neck while he is putting a young bird back into its nest."

Rachel laughed at this while his mother exclaimed: "How dare you talk like that, Richard!"

"He is only being a teaze," said Rachel, looking up at Anne. "I have got used to it now, and pay no attention to him."

"Finish the story, mother," said Richard, and Anne added her voice to his. "Please finish the story. I am waiting to hear how the house was burnt down. Then I shall go home and buy some fire extinguishers."

They all laughed at this, and Mrs. Sotheby continued:

"After Captain Purdue's death it was nearly a year before the lawyers could find the heirs to the estate, and when they did find them the trouble was to know what to do with them. They called themselves Putty, though the name was really Purdue; the father and mother were dead and there were two brothers and two sisters. They had lived all their lives in a tumble-down cottage without proper windows or doors, right out on the Bedford Level, miles from anywhere. The brothers were labourers, ditchers. The elder of the two was called Jack: he was the best of the family but it was difficult to make out what he said. There was no getting anything out of his brother; he was stone deaf and had a cleft palate. The girls were very wild, dirty creatures, and not quite right in the head. When they were sober they were all like wooden images, and they looked very queer when they first came, in the black clothes Mr. Stott had bought for them. Well, they moved into the house, and within a week all the servants left and they were alone there. None of the gentry round would have anything to do with them; nobody went near the house except Dr. Boulder and Mr. Noble, who was the vicar here in those days, and of course Mr. Stott, the lawyer. At first they lived very quietly, only making a fearful mess of the three rooms they used. They were afraid that Mr. Stott could turn them out if he had wanted to, but after they had been there two or three months they grew more confident. And though they were like images if there were other people about, there was plenty of noise when they were by themselves and when they were drunk. Jack used to throw things and his sisters would throw things back. At first they came to " The Red Cow " for drink, and Jack used sometimes to wave Captain Purdue's hunting crop and threaten to horsewhip anybody who didn't take his hat off, and one day when he had got very drunk he stood by the monument on the green and made a speech. People could hear him bellowing for miles round, but no one could make out much of what he said except that he was the squire, and that he ought to have been told before, and that he would never be rough with anybody.

"One day when he was in ' The Red Cow ' one of the men asked him how it was that he didn't like port wine. That was the first Jack had heard of Captain Purdue's cellar, for would you believe it, the Puttys had never been all over the house, and the cellar being locked up they had not troubled to break it open. After they found the wine nothing was seen of them for more than a week and then, one night, we were all woken up with the news that the manor house had caught fire. Everyone in the village turned out to help and the fire engine was fetched from Linton, but it came too late to be any use. The whole house was ablaze when we got there; the dairy and stables too, for they were touching the house. The men had made a line from the pond and were passing buckets, but it did no good, for the rooms were very old-fashioned and all the panelling had caught alight by that time, and the staircase too. The flames made it as light as day."

" What about the Puttys? " asked Anne.

" Well that was a very dreadful story. Jack Putty had just broken his way out of the house when we got there, but the two girls and the deaf brother were still inside. One of the Peck boys who went to Wet Coulter afterwards as a ploughman, got out both of the girls, but they were terribly burned, and the brother lost his life. Jack Putty did not seem to understand what was happening at first, but when the fire had taken hold of everything he missed his brother, and then he ran back into the house to find him. He came out again with his clothes alight and jumped into the pond, and then, when he got out, he ran back into the fire again. It was dreadful to see that. He got out alive a second time, and would have gone in a third time, but everyone could see it was no use, and they prevented him; it took four men to hold him. Poor fellow, his feet were terribly burned, but he didn't seem to mind that, but kept crying out that he must save his brother.

" After that they were all taken to the hospital, and there they found out that the girls were not fit to be about, so they were sent to an asylum for the imbecile. They have been there ever since, but Jack Putty seemed a different man after that. He went out to Australia; Mr. Stott sends him his rent regularly, and Jack sent him word when he got married. The property still belongs to him of course, and that is how it is that the manor house has never been rebuilt."

There was a silence in the little parlour, while they turned the story over in their minds. Mrs. Sotheby began to poke up the fire in the grate, and the flames shot up ; they had been sitting almost in the dark.

" A wonderful story," said Richard. " I often think of Jack Putty as a model: a man who was really able to love his brother as himself. That is the only sort of love, love which will sacrifice everything, put up with everything, yet ask for nothing in return. Selfish love is misery,

I suppose it deserves to be , but how does one avoid it? "

" Why do you think Jack Putty felt un-selfish love? " Anne asked, feeling rather puzzled.

" You don't think he tried to go back into the fire for the third time because it was gentlemanly, do you, though I've no doubt he really was a gentleman," answered Richard.

" You would not have thought Jack Putty was a gentleman if you had seen him," said his mother.

" I daresay not, but I should have been wrong . . . he was fearless, and he was independent," said Richard.

" He certainly was not a biddable man," said Mrs. Sotheby. " But that was the only thing he had in common with his second cousin, Captain Purdue."

" The Peck boy went in once, to rescue the two girls, but I should not have gone in at all. I don't think I should go into a burning house even if you or Rachel were inside it. I'm sure if Ginette . . . Grandison . . . But it's not a proof of love at all; some people will risk their lives to save a kitten." He muttered something else, but the others could not catch it.

"I must be going," said Anne, getting up. "Gracious me, it is past six o'clock." And thanking Mrs. Sotheby for her story and kissing Rachel, she hurried back through the rain to the vicarage to prepare supper.

Chapter 10

NO GOOD-BYES

It was morning before Anne could find any sleep, and the hours she spent lying in the darkness with her eyes open, or sometimes standing at her bedroom window gazing out at the pale lawn and the moony spaces of the orchard beyond, listening to the whispering notes of the little owls, and to the weather-vane on the dove house, whimpering as it swung in the wind: those hours were remembered afterwards as the most miserable of her life.

" What have I done? " she asked herself, but she could find nothing in her own conduct to explain Richard's behaviour. " If he regarded me with even the interest of a casual acquaintance he must have told me of his departure. He would have said something, surely. Even if he hates me he would have spoken of when he was going away."

But Richard had not mentioned it, and had it not been for a chance remark of Mr. Sotheby's she would have known nothing of the matter. " He must have intended to hide it from me," she said, wondering why it should be hidden and asking herself if it was because he was afraid of telling her, or because he had fancied that she was in love with him.

"No, he has no such thoughts," she assured herself. "It is because of his complete indifference to me. His whole mind is occupied by Ginette Grandison." And suddenly a new thought striking her, she said aloud and almost joyfully: "Who knows what unhappiness she may be causing him?" The thought of Richard's pain was a comfort to her, and she wondered once more what the woman could be like who had so enslaved him.

"I seem sometimes in my thoughts to assume that I am in love with Richard myself," she said to herself with surprise. "But indeed I don't love him. He is hateful; when I am with him I know well enough that we could never by any chance love each other. He is as sharp as his own nose; he has no feelings that I can understand. But yet I am fond of him, for he is the first man to whom I have been able to speak freely, the first man. How I long to live in a world of such men. To live in Paris."

Presently her thoughts turned from

148

Richard and his cruel behaviour, to think of her own life and what it would become.

"I should have escaped from here by now had it not been for him," she said bitterly, and then recollecting that there had been no more answers to her advertisement, she wondered if she would ever have another opportunity. "If I have the courage to advertise again," she added, for even that seemed doubtful to her at that hour.

"Damn the fellow," she said at last. "He has disturbed my life to no purpose, he has raised a hundred questions he cannot answer; I should have been happier if I had never seen him."

And it seemed to her that every fresh experience in life would always bring her such regrets; that all struggles were only destined to make her suffer, and that the best course perhaps was to go through life blindly, living from day to day, immersed in a world of dreams like her father, and like him shunning all contact with her fellow creatures. These thoughts were dreadful to her, for the afternoons she had passed sitting at the Burnt Farm talking to Richard Sotheby while he painted her were precious. "The happiest moments in my life," she cried. " For I thought then that I had found a friend."

Yet it was true: she would have been happier if she had never met him.

" I am not jealous," she exclaimed. " I know he is in love with Ginette Grandison I have always known it, and it has never given me a moment's pang of jealousy. If only he had spoken of her, if he had told me he was going back to her, I should have felt happy for his sake. I should not have had a single selfish thought.

" But he has made me lay bare my whole life to him and has never once spoken of his own. I only know of the existence of Ginette Grandison by an accident; he would not trust me with his secret and would be annoyed at my knowing it. No friendship can be based on anything so one-sided as our conversations have been. And the reason is plain, only that I have been too stupid to see it before. The reason is that he never intended a friendship. It amused him to get my little secret from me; it flattered his. . . ."

But Anne suddenly checked her thought crying: " No, that is vulgar, that is unworthy. The root of the matter is that I mean nothing to him, nothing, whilst to me he is the only man with whom I have spoken freely; the only intimate friend except Enid that I have ever had. And he cares no more for me than she did."

A flood of tears eased her heart; she turned her face to the pillow; then, when she had done weeping, she got out of bed once more and went to the window. The air was cold; there was a gust of wind in the chimney; the weather-cock gave its gentle whine.

After standing there an hour, Anne went back to bed again with a picture of the darkness in her mind, saying to herself: " And so on for ever and ever, cold and darkness after the sunshine and the warmth of the day."

Next morning Anne felt ill when she woke; her head ached, she was dizzy, and the outer world was seen alternately as a whirling mist and defined with extra-ordinary clearness. She got up from habit, but she could eat nothing at breakfast, and as soon as her bed had been made she undressed and lay down on it, and fell asleep.

When she awoke it was with the echo of Richard's voice ringing in her ears; she scrambled out of bed and went at

once to her window. There was nothing
to be seen, she blinked her eyes in the
brilliant sunlight, and reeling with sleep,
groped her way back through the sudden
darkness of the room to her bed to fall
into a doze from which she awoke once
more, this time with the certainty of
having heard voices: beyond a doubt, one
of them was Richard's.

The voices rose for a moment; then
she heard the front door slam, in a gust
of wind, and there was a silence. She
understood suddenly that Richard had
been in the house; that he had come to
see her, and she got out of bed.

The bedroom window gave onto the
garden, so she ran to her father's room
just as she had done to see the ploughmen
on that snowy winter morning. Her guess
had been right, for there almost directly
beneath her were Richard and her father;
they were standing bare-headed in the
rain talking amicably; she could hear her
father's gentle laugh; they were reluctant
to part. Anne's first instinct was to call
out; to ask Richard to wait while she exchanged her dressing-gown for clothes
in which she could appear, but she realised that it was impossible to do so, and

then, with the angry feelings that every sick person has experienced of knowing that life is going on unchanged behind his back, she was forced to watch Richard disappear after shaking hands with her father by the garden gate.

"A thousand pities," she said to herself. "He must have come to see me. What can he have said to my father?" Her headache and dizziness were gone, she felt eager and excited, and the moments while she was putting on her clothes and doing up her hair were spent in trying to imagine the conversation that had been going on while she was asleep.

"What an extraordinary thing," said Anne, "that he should think of calling! Nobody but Richard would have done such a thing!" Her thoughts were interrupted by Maggie coming to ask her if she would like to have tea in bed. As she was going downstairs it occurred to her that Richard might have spoken of her; he would have told her father that they had met; he might even have mentioned his picture. As she opened the door into the room where her father was already sitting, she remembered the well-brought up heroes in Victorian novels who ask a father's permission before entering into correspondence with the girl they have rescued when the pony has taken the bit between its teeth and the governess cart is heading for the side of the quarry . . . a memory which was driven away with a laugh, but which left her anxious and expectant as she took her place at the tea table.

Mr. Dunnock did not make any reference to his visitor, though he was less abstracted than usual, asking Anne with great solicitude about her headache, and then saying: " I have been feeling a little more melancholy than usual to-day because of the bad weather, and so I took down Burton. In his anatomy he has much to say about the effect of food. The authorities all agree that beef is only safe for those who lead an active life; that pork is definitely bad for the reasoning man; that goats' flesh disposes those who partake of it to evil-living; venison is most strongly condemned, and even horse-flesh is held to account for the well-known melancholy of your Spaniard; among vegetables the onion and its congeners, and I am glad to say the cabbage, are absolutely condemned; peas and beans should be avoided

154

as far as possible, and salads and fruit only taken in the strictest moderation. Burton thinks that the potato may be a safe article of diet, and highly recommends borage."

Anne was smiling at her father's enthusiasm. "There seems very little for you to eat," she said.

"Well Anne, I do not know quite what Burton would recommend; he says nothing against wheaten bread; he regards fresh country cheese as wholesome, and speaks with enthusiasm of beer." Mr. Dunnock giggled as he said this and for some reason that familiar clerical sound seemed to his daughter at that moment to express all that she most hated and despised. "The giggle is unforgivable," she said to herself gazing at her father over the tea-table. "He is a grown-up man; he has a beard; he is my father, but if beer is mentioned one hears a silly adolescent giggle. One would think that he was a choir boy caught with a cigarette."

She left the table and went out into the garden in a fury; she had forgotten her own embarrassment when Richard had used the word " rape."

155

Mr. Dunnock, absorbed in his own thoughts, hardly looked after her.

"Beer," he said, pouring himself out a fourth cup of tea, and giggling slightly. "Good stuff, beer. He thought that because his name was Burton," and Mr. Dunnock began to wonder if Robert Burton had really come from Burton-on Trent, and if beer had always been brewed there.

"I forgot to tell you," he said to Anne at supper, "that I had a visit this afternoon from Richard Sotheby, the son of our grocer. It was a great pity that you had a headache for we do not have many interesting visitors. I think he is charming: a most delightful, most intelligent young man. But you should have told me that you had met him; you should have asked him to tea, and have introduced him to me. It was too bad, Anne, to have kept him to yourself."

Anne gasped with astonishment, and not knowing what to reply, waited until her father went on: "He seems to have liked you very much; you have made quite a conquest," and Mr. Dunnock smiled his peculiar little smile which showed that he was not speaking seriously.

" I thought you rather disapproved of the Sothebys," said Anne. " Because, of course, they are Nonconformists."

" Well, well," said her father, wrinkling up his face at the word, for it set his teeth on edge like the thought of sour fruit. " Well, well, I suppose they are happy with their little ugly worship; I confess their outlook is repugnant to me. But the son has escaped from all that. He told me he has been to visit Little Gidding, and asked me a number of questions about Nicholas Ferrar's community. Apparently he is greatly interested in the antiquities of the county."

Anne had known Little Gidding all her life, and she shared her father's love for the lonely little church perched on the edge of the hillside, with the slope of green sward below and the woods behind. She had been brought up to revere Nicholas Ferrar, and had loved to reconstruct a life which had so much of the beauty of religion in it, and nothing of what she disliked. Often she thought that she would have been content for her father to have been a clergyman if he had lived in the seventeenth century, or even in the eighteenth for the matter of that, for it was only during the reign of Queen Victoria that the clergy in England lost touch with the community and became self-conscious. Anne knew how much happier her father would have been had he belonged to Nicholas Ferrar's household, and though she would not have cared for it herself (she would have disliked rising at four o'clock for prayers every morning) she wished he could live in such a way himself. Thus for once she was tolerant, for she loved Little Gidding, and had prayed in the narrow little church with an outburst of religious passion such as she had never experienced in Ely Cathedral.

For the rest of that evening father and daughter spoke of Little Gidding, calling up pictures in each other's minds of how it must be looking in the spring weather, and of the life of the immense and extraordinary household which had lived there until the Roundheads had burned the roof over their heads and had thrown the brass eagle lectern in the church into the pond below.

" The men slept in one wing of the house and the women in the other," Anne remembered. " And Nicholas Ferrar slept watchfully in the middle. That is the funny side," but she hid her thought from her father, and when she spoke it was to remind him of the immense number of children in the community.

" His daughter brought her eleven children; there were thirty people altogether," said her father, and he passed on to describe the three visits of King Charles I, and so vivid were his words that Anne could picture to herself, more clearly than ever before, the visit the King paid during the civil war when he came toiling up the hill on foot, and alone, to pray.

" There is no more sacred spot in England," said Mr. Dunnock, and Anne was inclined to agree with him. That night she lay for some time without sleeping, giving herself up to the happiest thoughts, and when at last she dozed off it was with the picture of Richard Sotheby in her mind: Richard walking over the greenest turf where the manor house had stood, resting on the sides of the dry grassy moat, and then walking down by the edge of the wood to the little church with Nicholas Ferrar's tomb in the pathway leading up to it, under a tombstone, the letters of which are written in moss. A

tall figure came toiling up the hill to meet
him; she saw a tired man with a pale face
—King Charles the First, and try how she
would to dream of Richard Sotheby, King
Charles would reappear.

"I shall certainly try to see Richard
before he goes this morning," Anne
thought at breakfast. "I shall look in and
tell Mrs. Sotheby that I have come to say
good-bye."

But when the time came she went past
the shop, for she remembered Mr. Sotheby's look of surprise when he found that
she was acquainted with his son, and the
long hostile silence before he spoke, after
he had recognised her in the painting.

"Mr. Sotheby does not approve of
my knowing Richard," Anne said to herself, glancing through the windows of
the shop. She could see no one inside,
and the longer she meditated over the
grocer's behaviour at Rachel's birthday
party, the more convinced she became that
he was jealous of her, and alarmed lest an
attachment should spring up between his
son and her.

"I will go for a stroll on the green,"
and looking about her she saw for the
first time that the sun was shining, and

that the grass was greener after the rain of the day before. " Why the hawthorns have come into leaf; the horse-chestnut buds are bursting; in a few days the apples will be in blossom," but the daily progress of the spring, which would ordinarily have given her such keen pleasure, was meaningless now. " I must see Richard before he goes," she said in desperation. " I must arrange with him about finding me work in Paris," and she remembered with dismay that she did not even know his address.

Soon she turned back on her footsteps, and fully an hour was spent in passing and repassing the grocer's shop.

" I am wasting my time," she thought. " For Easter is nearly upon us; there is much to do at the church." But it was not possible to go home after waiting so long, and at last she set off along the road to Linton. A mile was covered before it occurred to her that Richard would be driving with his father, and that even if Mr. Sotheby should pull up it would be difficult for them to speak in front of him, and she turned back and walked to the village at top speed.

All seemed well, for she had not passed

them on the road, and she determined once more to enter the shop, but it occurred to her, as she approached, that Rachel would be coming out of school in a few minutes: it was just twelve o'clock.

As she turned the corner by the schoolhouse, she noticed the strange ring deeply cut into the earth and full of dust, and wondered again what game the children played there.

Soon the door opened and the children began to run out. " In this riot I shall not be able to speak to Rachel," Anne said to herself. " But if I walk back towards the shop she may walk another way."

"A lovely morning, Miss Dunnock," said a voice behind her, and she turned to find Mr. Lambert.

The moments spent talking to him were agonising, for every instant she expected to see Rachel run past her, but Mr. Lambert would not be hurried. Soon he began to speak of Easter, and the arrangements at the church, for he was a churchwarden, and when that subject was exhausted he returned to the weather.

" One is happy to be alive on such a morning, Miss Dunnock; I envy you your leisure to enjoy it. Free as air, Miss

Dunnock, and no one to call your master. Work is my master. This weather keeps us very busy."

"Impertinent puppy," said Anne to herself, though as a matter of fact she rather liked Mr. Lambert, and saw nothing impertinent in his manners.

At the very moment when Mr. Lambert released her she heard Rachel's voice saying: "Good morning, Miss Dunnock," and the little girl ran by her with two or three other children. Anne saw that it was useless to wait any longer, and returned to the vicarage; there was nothing to be angry about, nobody was at fault.

"There was this note left for you. Rachel Sotheby brought it over," said Maggie when she went into the kitchen, and Anne thought the girl's grin was an impertinence too.

Richard had gone by the early morning train. "I am so sorry not to see you to say good-bye," he wrote. "You must not forget your promise to write, and remember to tell me all the news of the parish." He enclosed his address.

Chapter 11

BEFORE THE SWALLOW

EASTER was over, but the church at Dry Coulter was still full of the scent of flowers mingled with the odour of their corruption. A necklace of decayed marsh mallows hung forlornly round the neck of the eagle; its brazen beak held a bunch of wilted cowslips, but the daffodils and narcissus on the altar still breathed out their perfume. Easter was over, and Mr. Dunnock heaved a sigh of relief, for he had come to feel the church festivals a great strain upon him.

Easter was over; Mrs. Pattle marched up the aisle on her flat feet and began tearing down the flowers which her children had gathered three days before.

Mr. Dunnock walked by the little pathway from the vestry to his wife's grave, and stood there looking at the headstone. He stayed there so long and stood so still that a robin, recognising a friend in him, came to perch on his shoulder.

" The resurrection of the flesh has come to pass," Mr. Dunnock said aloud. " These ones come to me and they com-

164

mune with me; why does she alone delay?"

At last a cow lowing on the other side of the hedge, interrupted the clergyman's reverie; he started slightly and coming to himself began to pull his beard with a gesture of despair, and the robin, who had been wondering if he could induce his wife to nest in it, flew off to a tombstone, disappointed.

"I live in two worlds," Mr. Dunnock reflected. "Only the saints know how terrible the strain of such an experience can be. I cannot bear it much longer; something will break in me. My head aches when I am recalled from the contemplation of so much glory to the pettiness in which men live, their eyes on the ground and their ears stopped to the voices of the angels. I cannot endure it any longer; it would be better I think if I were to live alone." He clutched at his head suddenly, and then walked rapidly from the churchyard towards the vicarage. But the song of a willow wren caught his ear as he passed under the elms, and he paused to listen. The clear top note was followed by a stream of softer sounds and ended with a cadence of lower notes, a touch of melancholy in which the vicar felt his own heart expressed. The bird sang, and sang again and Mr. Dunnock, resting his shoulder against the rough bark of an elm, listened without seeing the approach of two village women, or noticing their inquisitive glances as they passed near him, or hearing their words, for, in answer to a nudge, one of them had protested to her companion: " Oh, dear me, Fanny. Don't."

They were silent for fear of laughing, but when they had passed the vicar, one of them said: "Maggie told me she couldn't make anything of his sermon on Easter Sunday. It was all about Easter Eggs being the promise of glory. She didn't know what he meant by it."

But the women did not laugh, and soon turned to safer and more interesting topics of conversation.

The willow wren had been silent a long while, and was looking for worms, when at last for Mr. Dunnock also the mood of ecstasy passed; he looked about him startled and bewildered, and then, reassured by finding he was alone, he shook his head sadly, and the first glance of fear was replaced by a bitter smile as he hurried back to the vicarage at top speed.

" Lay my meals on a tray in future,"
he said to Maggie a few minutes later.
" And put the tray on the table in the
passage outside my study. I shall hear if
you tap on the door." Words which were
repeated to Anne when she came down
to lunch. She was content to be alone,
but at dinner she was disturbed at this
alteration in her father's habits, wondering
whether he were unwell, or whether by any
chance Maggie were right in believing that
he wished the change to be permanent.
But this seemed to her so unlikely a pos-
sibility that she did not dwell on it, and,
when the meal was over, she lit the lamp
and settled down with her drawing-board
in front of her; she had at last begun the
fashion plates which she had been projecting all the winter. The fine weather
had returned after Richard Sotheby's
departure, and for the first day of warm
sunshine Anne had found happiness
enough in being out of doors, a happiness shot through with irritation against
herself.

" I am wasting my life looking at this
pear blossom. What does it matter to me
whether the fruit set or not? I shall be gone
before the gathering." But her habitual

interest had been too strong for her, and she had watched the bees flying in and out among the masses of curdy petals with delight.

"I am lingering on. I shall linger all my life. I must go now; I must leave home to-day."

But it was impossible to leave on the day before Easter, and instead of packing her box, she had gone to the church to pin up the notice saying: "There will be no service on Saturday, when the church will be open for decoration."

When Saturday had come she had gone herself to help the little girls, and it was not until after Easter was over that the fashion plates had been begun. The results of her labours surpassed Anne's expectations; such fashion plates as hers she felt sure would excite the Parisian dressmakers.

"I must send them to Richard at once," she said as she took out the drawing pins. But the thought of waiting for a letter, and the agony of uncertainty in which she saw herself, dismayed her. In her mood of exultation delay of any kind seemed impossible.

"But I will wait all the same," she said,

" until I have finished a dozen, and then I shall go to Paris myself to seek my fortune. I will write and tell Richard that I am coming."

The letter was put off; she would not write until she knew the day and the hour of her arrival, and for several days she worked hard, shutting herself up in her room every morning when the bed had been made. When she laid down her brush it was to plan how she would have her hair cut off in London, and how she would buy herself a smart dress for the journey, for she believed that she would never impress a dressmaker in such rags as she possessed. With her mind full of such matters, Anne rose and looked out of her window; the first blush of pink petals was showing through the early green of the apple trees; in another week they would be in full blossom. Under the trees Mr. Dunnock was standing with his arms raised above his head, gazing up at the sky, a pose which Anne found sufficiently startling to make her look again, carefully screening her eyes from the sunlight. Her father stood motionless; every little while she could see a small bird fly up and settle on his shoulder.

" I have scarcely spoken to father for three days; I must speak to him now and tell him of my plans," and as she made this resolution, she saw him moving slowly across the lawn. As he came nearer she saw that a crowd of little birds was following him, a wild twittering came from them, they were mobbing him as though he were a cat or an owl; at every moment birds would settle on his head or shoulders, or on his upraised hands, and then would fly off again.

A beautiful spectacle it seemed to Anne, and she felt a new tenderness for her father as she watched. The thin black figure with the head thrown back, the eyes turned up, and the beard jutting out, no longer seemed queer as it had a moment before, when she had first caught sight of it standing under the apple trees.

" He will feel my desertion," she murmured, a sudden sympathy with her father coming to her, and she felt a love which had been forgotten for many months.

" First mother, and then me," she said. But her love did not weaken her determination to speak to him of her departure, but strengthened it.

When Mr. Dunnock reached the house,

he shook his head, first gently, but then, as a blue-tit still remained perched there, more violently, and then turning round waved his hands towards the birds which had settled in the rose bushes about the door. Anne saw that he was bestowing a benediction. She did not wait longer, but hurrying downstairs, followed her father into his study.

" We see very little of each other now, father," she said.

Mr. Dunnock started at her words and looked round at her with guilty eyes.

" Yes, Anne, yes," he murmured. " Do you wish to speak to me? Something perhaps about the housekeeping? " and he began to fidget with his fingers, wishing that she would go away.

" I have wanted to speak to you for some time," said Anne. " I have been thinking a great deal about my own life. It will seem very selfish to you, and very heartless. It is very selfish. . . ."

" We are all of us selfish," said Mr. Dunnock. " What is it that you want? "

" I want to go away, at least for a time," said Anne. " I do not want to settle down for the rest of my life without seeing something of the world. I have never been to London."

There was a silence, and after a little she went on: "I shall have to earn my own living of course, but that should not be impossible. An experiment . . . an experience . . . the experience would be good for me. I have never been to London. There are so many things."

"That seems a very sensible plan, if it can be managed," said Mr. Dunnock, cutting her short. "But then you have plenty of good sense, Anne, more than I have in some ways."

He sat down suddenly at his writing table, dropping his head between his hands, and there he remained, silent for so long that Anne began to wonder if he had forgotten her, but she said nothing, only repeating under her breath: "It is settled: I am leaving home."

But at last Mr. Dunnock looked up, saying: "Let me see . . . What was I going to say? You will require some money, Anne, if you are going away. I can give you twenty pounds, enough to enable you to look about you. Do as you think best, dear child, in every way." His head began to nod again, and then, as if suddenly waking up, he said:

"I am glad you are going, Anne. I

am glad the suggestion came from you: that it should be your own wish. I am rather bad company, I know, but there is a reason for that. You think my life here is narrow perhaps, but you see only one side. I can assure you that you are mistaken; my life is incredibly rich and overflowing with happiness. But that has to be hidden; there is a reason for that. I need loneliness; you perhaps need to see the world at present, but we shall meet again, and I have no fear that ultimately . . . you will understand what is hidden. . . ." he broke off disconnectedly, and suddenly Anne felt her happiness shot through by a feeling of dismay, in which she wondered if she could leave her father to fend for himself. Such phrases were familiar to her from his lips, but they seemed strange coming at such a moment and when she went from the room it was with a conviction that she would be doing wrong to go away.

Her scruples were soon forgotten in the excitement of making plans, and the rest of the day was spent in packing and unpacking a wooden box with her possessions. Two days later all was ready, and the hour of her departure had been fixed for the morrow. In the morning she went to say good-bye to Mrs. Sotheby, and to ask if Rachel would come to have tea with her.

" We shall miss you very much," said Mrs. Sotheby. " But I shall try to think that you are enjoying yourself seeing more of the world than you would here. I hardly know what to say about Rachel. You know how fond she is of you. She will want to come to say goodbye; it is a great pity that Mr. Sotheby has arranged to take us to see the cottages at Linton. You would not care to come with us, I suppose? Then everyone would be happy."

" I should like to come very much," said Anne, " if I shall not be in the way."

" I'll just ask Mr. Sotheby if there will be room in the dog-cart for us all," said the old woman and, through the opened door into the parlour, Anne could see the grocer sitting at the table, looking up from a sheet of blue paper with a T-square in his hands.

They set off soon after lunch, Anne sitting on the back seat of the dog-cart with Rachel, but the pony did not seem to feel the extra weight. Anne soon set Rachel talking, and the little girl kept her amused with stories of her school, and how she had been teazed about her brother, and it was some time before she broke the news of her own departure. Rachel stared down at the road, a yellow river flowing so swiftly from below the dog-cart that she could not distinguish the stones in it. "You won't ever think of me; you won't write to me; you won't ever come back," were her thoughts but she knew that she must hide her unhappiness, and when she spoke, as the trap drew up smartly, it was to ask: "Will you be going to Paris?" a question which Anne found so disturbing that she saw little of the first cottage into which she was led. The smell of fresh paint, mingled with the fragrance of aromatic pine shavings on the plank floors, recalled her to her surroundings, and she listened for a moment to Mr. Sotheby who was speaking to her.

"These cottages are only a stepping-stone to greater things, Miss Dunnock. I have mortgaged them already. What Linton lacks is a high-class Temperance Hotel, overlooking the river. Such a hotel would attract visitors for the fishing and boating, and would cater also for the more respectable commercial men. A Temperance Hotel would wake up trade in the town, and would provide a delightful centre for holiday-makers and abstainers, and men from the university."

" What shall I say to Rachel? " Anne asked herself as she followed the grocer up the little staircase into the pokey bedrooms, which smelt of varnish.

" A little shop like ours is a great snare for a man with ambition. I have wasted the best years of my life in it, years during which I might have built up a great merchandising house. But this hotel, and others like it, will soon make my son a rich man, and provide for Rachel. A Temperance Hotel with a grand loggia looking over the river, pillars with climbing roses, a small winter garden with azaleas. . . . We must move with the times, you know, Miss Dunnock."

Anne descended the narrow stairs and followed Mrs. Sotheby across a patch of sticky clay to the dog-cart.

" Yes, I am going to Paris. Don't tell anyone; it is a secret," she said to the little girl as they drove off. It was only after saying this that Anne looked up at the cottages, seeing them for the first time.

Their extreme ugliness and the evident signs of jerry-building dismayed her.

"What will the next thing be like?" she asked herself, remembering the grocer had spoken of an hotel, and expecting to see it round the corner. In a moment or two Mr. Sotheby drew rein by the side of the quiet stream of the Ouse, but there was no building visible, only an empty field, the site for the new hotel.

"A lounge hall lit entirely by windows of yellow stained glass is my idea," said Mr. Sotheby. "It will give the effect of sunshine all the year round. The landing-stage is to run the entire length of the building. It will be covered by a glass roof. There is to be a garage on the right and a boathouse on the left, each under its own dome of glass, thus giving symmetry to the whole. There will be central heating, a lift, electric light, a banqueting hall. . . ."

Anne gazed at the water-logged field, at the slow stream with the bunches of reeds and the gasworks on the opposite bank, and ceased to listen to Mr. Sotheby's words. The mud and water and slime would remain mud and water and slime; the fine old bridge with the toll house, which had once been a chapel, would stay there; nothing would move the gasworks, and Anne felt unable to picture to herself the glittering abomination of which the grocer spoke, on that melancholy river bank.

But Mr. Sotheby went on talking for some time, and, turning her head, Anne could see that his wife was not listening, and her own attention soon wandered. She saw the whip being pointed first in one direction and then in another, and the white beard which wagged as the grocer opened and shut his mouth, but the stream of words went on unheard. At last Mr. Sotheby picked up the reins, cracked his whip and they set off for home. Except for Rachel, they had enjoyed themselves as Mrs. Sotheby had predicted.

No one in Dry Coulter would have recognised the slim figure in a fashionable tailor-made dress who took her seat in the boat-train three days later. When she shook her head to refuse the offer of magazines, no hairpins flew onto the platform, and the reason was explained when she removed her rakish little hat: Anne wore an Eton crop. Her whole character seemed to her to have changed, and looking into the mirror in the lid of her little vanity-case, she was pleased with her new self. For a moment she fingered an unused lip-stick and then, laughing to herself, deliberately reddened her lips. She was off to Paris, alone, to seek her fortune. Her father, everyone at Dry Coulter, every experience she had ever had in her life seemed never to have existed. It was a dream which would be speedily forgotten, and reaching for her bag, Anne opened a French book of which Richard had spoken.

Somewhere in the Weald of Kent, the grinding noise of the brakes, suddenly applied, disturbed her reading. The train dragged itself to a halt and a long silence followed.

At last Anne threw open the window and peered into the darkness. There was nothing to be seen but a red light shining somewhere down the line, and the vague forms of oak trees near at hand. For a moment there was nothing to be heard, and then, suddenly, her ear caught a far-off melodious chuckle and a moment afterwards the first startling clear notes of a bird's song. The red light changed to green; there was a long puff, and a series of snorts from the engine; the ticking of released brakes, and once more the train was in motion. But Anne had recognised the note of the nightingale.

" Love," she said to herself, and began laughing.

Chapter 12

RICHARD'S FRIENDS

Two men and a woman were having breakfast in the studio in their dressing-gowns.

"Oh, my God, Grandison!" exclaimed Richard Sotheby, after looking into the letter which Anne had posted two days before in London. "What am I to do?" Here is that girl arriving in Paris to-morrow. She asks me to get her lodgings, and to meet her at the station. What on earth am I to do? I wonder if I could stop her coming. . . . She doesn't give her London address. No, I can't stop her. Oh, what a curse. . . ."

Grandison laughed and, turning to the woman beside him, told her the news in bad French. A look of incredulity passed over her brown face, and then she also began to laugh. The dark eyes sparkled with malice, the even white teeth shone, she put the point of her healthy pink tongue between her painted lips; and then, the humour of the situation increasing as she turned the news over in her mind, she sprang up and danced bare-footed round the breakfast table in the middle of the immense room. The skirts of the silk dressing-gown whirled round the lithe body; every movement was lovely, but neither of the men looked at her. When she stopped it was to pour out a flood of questions which went unanswered.

" It is not a joke," said Richard Sotheby gloomily. " You will have to help me. You don't object, I suppose," he added in French to the girl, " if Grandison devotes his time to her? "

" How insolent you are, Richard! " said the woman, taking hold of Grandison's arm, and putting her cheek beside his head. " I am to be sacrificed because you can't face a woman. I could call you some hard names if I chose." She pouted, but at once went on: " But I won't for I sympathise with you. Really I am anxious to see this girl of yours, Richard. It will be a curiosity. Are you going to bring her to live with us? I shall be charming to her, and she will keep me company sometimes. Two men is more than I can manage." She pouted again, and added in tones of deep tenderness: " Two dirty Englishmen."

Richard Sotheby looked at her with a

patient smile, then, ignoring her questions, he turned to his friend and said, speaking in English: " And two women is more than I can manage."

Grandison flushed with anger, but Richard forestalled anything he might have said by adding: " My dear you know I am fond of Ginette; don't misunderstand what I say. But two women is more than I can put up with. . . . "

" Why on earth will you persist in regarding Ginette as a woman? " demanded the younger man in tones of fury. "Woman! woman! It's always woman with you. Ginette is Ginette, just as I am Gerald and you are Richard."

Sotheby did not reply, and his friend's angry tones soon subsided. Harmony was restored while the breakfast dishes were cleared away, and for the rest of the morning Anne's arrival was discussed calmly, sometimes in English, sometimes in French, while the two men painted and Ginette posed. In the evening everything that had been said in the morning was repeated, but at last it was decided that Grandison should meet Anne at the station, instead of Richard, and that he should take her to an hotel.

"Let it be on the other side of Paris," said Richard next morning, as he and Grandison left the studio on their way to the station, for he had decided to accompany his friend in order to point out the girl whom he was to meet.

"Everything in France is different," Anne said to herself as she looked out of the window of the train. "Those trees must be elms but they have been shaved like French poodles so that they are scarcely recognisable. These are fields of corn, and here are cocks and hens and cart-sheds, but they do not seem to be the real things so much as imitations of ours. And the houses! How extraordinarily different are the houses!" for the train was passing through a station, and building after building flashed by her: dreary houses with the stucco peeling off them, each with its broken slatted shutters beside the windows, houses such as do not exist in England.

"If there is any beauty in this country it is of another kind from our English beauty, just as the ugliness is unlike our ugliness." The change did not dismay her; it had the same effect of strangeness as the reflection of her own cropped head in the glass, seen unexpectedly as she lifted her handbag from off the luggage rack.

The train was approaching Paris, and before many minutes had passed a porter in a blue blouse had seized upon her handbag and Anne forgot to look for Richard Sotheby in the effort to produce a good impression on the porter. But even the inadequacy of her French could not detain him for more than a moment. His moustache trembled eagerly, his eye flashed, then he had disappeared.

" What a lovely outline there is to his cheek, how clear his complexion, how expressive his every movement! " and looking after the porter she began to fancy that if all Frenchmen were as handsome as the porter she would be in love with them all. " The beauty of the French face," she said, " lies in the beauty of the cheekbones. An English face is made up of eyes and nose and mouth: the rest of the face is a blank space, but take away a Frenchman's eyes: so often like eggs, or olives, take away his nose, and his mouth (always an uninteresting mouth) and you find his face is still full of expression and of beauty, indeed the face is improved."

But the porter was back, and had set

off down the platform with a command-
ing gesture to Anne to follow him, when
she found herself being accosted by a
stranger.

"Is this Miss Dunnock? My name's
Grandison," he said. "Richard Sotheby
asked me to meet you here; he is not able
to come himself. . . ."

"Ginette Grandison's brother," Anne
said to herself, looking into the surly,
boyish face, and noticing Grandison's shyness. Meanwhile the porter with the lovely
cheekbones had disappeared with her suit-
case.

"What does the porter matter?" she
thought. "What does the suit-case matter?
What does it matter what this young man
is mumbling about Richard? No, nothing
matters. This is Paris; I have arrived, and
a delightful happy life awaits me with
these charming people. The opera . . .
friends." In such a mood it seemed scarcely
surprising that Richard should after all
come up to them just as they were climbing into a cab.

"What is the latest news from Dry
Coulter?" he asked, taking the seat beside
her. Anne had not slept; the channel
crossing by night was too exciting an

experience to be missed, and she had remained on deck, watching the receding lights of England disappear, and then the lights of France springing up out of the darkness and growing in brilliance and in number.

" Dry Coulter? " she asked, and for the first moment the name conveyed nothing to her. " How can you ask about Dry Coulter when we are in Paris! " Richard laughed and Anne added at once: " Oh, I went with your father and mother and Rachel to see the new cottages, and the site for the hotel."

" What hotel? " asked Richard, but while Anne was explaining she did not notice the look of anxiety on his face, for she was too much taken up with looking out of the taxi window. Soon she was asking questions: " What is that building? that street? that monument? " and was astonished that neither Richard nor his friend could tell her. She would have liked to have spent hours driving about Paris, feeling Mr. Grandison's gaze fixed upon her, and aware of the slight flush on her own cheek, but suddenly they rattled over a bridge and had turned into a narrow lane.

187

"I have taken a room for you here," said Richard as they drew up. "You get your breakfast in your room, and an evening meal for about four shillings a day. I took it for a week. I suppose you will be staying a week in Paris."

"I shall be staying for ever," answered Anne.

Grandison gave a short, loud laugh. "I like the way you said that," he exclaimed, handing her suit-case out of the cab.

A sleepy-looking man had opened the hotel door, and was taking her luggage.

"We'll call for you this evening, and take you out to dinner if that would suit you," said Richard; and the next moment the taxi began to move off and she found herself alone.

"I shall like Mr. Grandison," she said as she followed the doorkeeper upstairs, and the excitement of looking at her room was mingled with the excitement of imagining that in a few days she would be laughing with the handsome man who had met her, and that he would lose his surliness and his shyness as they walked through Paris side by side. By the time she had finished unpacking she felt tired, and she lay down on the bed to rest. She could not sleep, and an hour later, when she looked out of the window she saw that the sunlight, which had greeted her on her arrival, had given place to driving rain. She had no umbrella, nor mackintosh, so she could not go out, and she felt shy and uncomfortable as she walked through the passages of the hotel. When she tried to speak to the chambermaid she found that she had forgotten her few words of French, but at last the day passed by and she was called from her room to find Mr. Grandison waiting for her in the hall.

"Richard sent me: he will meet us in the restaurant," he said. They got into a cab for it was still raining, and drove in silence until Anne, looking out of the window, asked what street they were in. "I don't know," answered the young man. "There are so many streets in Paris. But it is quite easy to find one's way about."

Anne would have liked to have asked him about his sister, but she lacked the courage and nothing more was said. The restaurant to which they had driven was like a hundred others which they had passed on the way, and appeared indistinguishable from the restaurants on either side of it; each with basket-work chairs heaped upside down on the little iron tables outside, with an awning flapping in the wind, and " Brasserie " written in gigantic letters along the front. It was still raining, but when they had passed through the doors they found the room was crowded.

Richard was waiting for them at a corner table, and they sat down. Soon food was brought them, and Richard began to speak about the restaurant, but Anne hardly took in his words and forgot to help herself from the little dishes, for she was charmed by the scene before her: the small tables, each with its merry party, men laughing hastily before filling their mouths with soup, swallowing it, and then laughing again as they tore the long rolls of bread to pieces with their fingers.

But Richard was pressing Anne to help herself, handing her the little dishes and filling her glass with yellow wine, then turning and speaking to Grandison about some play of Ibsen's which was being acted at a theatre in Paris. Anne's pleasure was increased by knowing that Richard and his friend were talking of a play which she had read, and that she could share in the discussion if she chose, but her attention wandered once more, and she was the first to notice a girl who came towards them threading her way between the tables, followed by a fat man with a square red beard, who stopped to speak to some acquaintances who hailed him as he passed. But the girl came on and held out a cool brown hand for Anne to shake.

" Mademoiselle Lariboisière—always called Ginette," said Richard. Ginette was beautiful, very beautiful, and Anne wondered how the mistake had arisen which had made her expect Ginette to be Mr. Grandison's sister. Instead of that she was a Frenchwoman with a lean brown face like a mask and dark hazel eyes with black lashes.

" If I were only like Ginette," she thought, a wish that recurred for many days afterwards whenever she was in her company, never guessing that the French girl was saying to herself: " If I were only like this English girl of Richard's! "

Ginette sat down opposite them without appearing surprised that Richard and Gerald should go on talking in English and pay no attention to her, interrupting each other, laughing at one moment and becoming almost angry in the next. But though they were talking in English, Anne did not listen either; she gazed across the table at Ginette, wishing that she could speak to her and get to know her. At last the meal was over, the dishes were cleared away and soon they were joined by the fat man, in spite of all appearances an American.

Anne found that he was kissing her hand, and a drop of soup from his beard was smeared over her fingers. Her face showed her disgust as she jumped up from her seat and without speaking to the American, who had drawn a chair near her, she went over to Ginette. But Ginette did not understand English, and after one or two halting sentences Anne fell into silence.

The group round the table was joined by several people, and each newcomer shook hands all round the table before sitting down. Anne had never shaken hands so often in her life, but there was no more hand-kissing and there were no more beards. A Chinaman seated himself beside Ginette, and they spoke so slowly

that Anne was able to follow their conversation; and she was astonished that
she had heard everything they said on the
lips of English curates at tea parties in
English parsonages. After a little while
Grandison came and sat beside her and
poured her out a glass of something warm,
perfumed and sticky; it seemed the most
delicious liquid that she had ever tasted.
Conversation flowed on all sides of
her, but she sat quiet, saying nothing
and looking at the pink face and the fair
hair of Richard's friend and then at the
Chinaman, who was talking so quietly
and so tediously about the fatigues of
railway journeys to Ginette, both of them
indifferent to the shouting, excited group
clustered round Richard and the red-
bearded American. Anne did not gather
what the subject of their argument was
and she felt no desire to do anything. An
hour passed and then another hour, and
once Grandison called to the waiter, who
refilled her little glass with the liqueur.
It was enough for her to know that she
was in Paris, and that this was her welcome. The voices, the faces, the Chinaman and Ginette melted into a dream full
of colour and of movement and shot

through with music; her head nodded and when Grandison touched her on the shoulder she smiled at him and realised that she was very tired.

"I want to go to bed," she said. "Will you please tell me the address of my hotel?"

"I'll see you home," he said. "Richard is set now; he will stay here for hours."

It had stopped raining, and they walked. The streets gleamed, and they turned into a great open place filled with trees and people sauntering under them. Men in groups were talking and laughing, pretty girls and painted women flashed their golden teeth as they passed by.

"How beautiful a town is," Anne said, almost unconscious that she was speaking aloud. "But I shall never be at home in one. The stones of the streets frighten me. I love the garden where:

> Stumbling on melons as I pass
> Insnared with flowers, I fall on grass,
> Annihilating all that's made
> To a green thought in a green shade."

She paused for a moment, stumbled with sleepiness and took Grandison's arm.

"The crowd here is so thick," she continued. "The faces search one's face, the eyes meet one's eyes, yet they all seem to be looking for someone they can never find."

They walked on slowly for some way in silence, but at last she spoke again.

" I believe everyone here is pursuing a dream, just as I pursued a dream walking under the elms at home; they speak to each other and pass on, but they never know each other. Man is always alone. They speak to each other, their eyes meet and sparkle; they smile and take each other by the arm: all in a dream. Here am I walking beside you, both of us are dreaming, unable to awake or to speak to each other." There was a pause; Grandison did not contradict what she had said, and then she murmured, more to herself than to him: " I am utterly alone, but so is everybody else."

They continued walking for a long way through deserted streets. Anne was feeling depressed by her train of thought, and Grandison was silent, but when at last they reached the Rue de Beaune she felt as if he had spoken and she had understood.

They shook hands, he looked into her eyes, cleared his throat as if he were going to speak, swallowed something, but then turned away without a word.

" I was wrong," Anne said, feeling her heart filled once more with hope. " There is patience and nobility and honesty and faithfulness in the world." As she dropped asleep it seemed to her that these qualities were inseparable from blue eyes and fair hair and fresh, blunt features.

Chapter 13

PARIS

Next day, when she got up, Anne said to herself that she must see Richard at once to discuss her plans with him. But the beauty of the day tempted her to explore Paris. The morning was spent happily in looking into the windows of the shops in the Rue de Rivoli and in buying herself an umbrella; then she lunched alone, thinking that it would be better to reach the studio in the afternoon. But it was already late before she found Montmartre, and when at last she had mounted the staircase and had rung the bell she was prepared for Richard to be out.

"A day wasted," she said to herself, but in her heart she felt that it had been well-spent, wishing that she could spend another day and then another in wandering about Paris. In the evening she had dinner at her hotel, and then went out once more to see the town by night.

"I can never get lost in Paris so long as I can find the river, for if I follow the river sooner or later I must come to the Pont Royal, and from there it is but a step to my hotel." She walked along the quays for some little way, but the Place de la Concorde tempted her with its wide expanse, and presently she found herself under the trees of the Champs Elysees. The clouds parted and the moonlight shone through the young leaves, a few dark figures moved in the shadows, and a band of young men passed her humming a foxtrot. Anne stopped for a moment and waved her arms with a sense of freedom and then strode rapidly up the hill.

At the Etoile she turned to the left down an avenue, which she guessed would bring her to the river, and when she saw the moonlight shining over the water she cried aloud: " I am free. I can do what I like; I can live how I like. I may never see Richard or his friend or anyone I have ever met again. I have no friends in the world. Nobody can interfere now with my happy life! " And suddenly, as she gazed over the water, Anne remembered how she had wept in her bedroom on the morning when the ploughmen had come. " No need for tears now that the accursed chain is broken. Who would guess, meeting me here, that I was the vicar's daughter with no hope of escaping from the parish? I am still alone, absolutely alone, but I care nothing for that because I am free. I am free!" she repeated in a loud voice which startled her, but there was no one near her, and she set off along the bank of the river. "I shall never go back!" she said, drawing herself up proudly, then, looking at the water, she wished that she could bathe, and her gaiety and irresponsibility were such that she was almost on the point of undressing beneath a lamp-post and plunging in. She recollected in time that she would be saved by a French policeman and walked on laughing as she pictured to herself the explanations that she would offer next morning in the police-court in her broken French.

"Richard would never forgive me if I dragged him to a police-court," she said, and her thoughts went back to her father. "Strange how blind I was thinking that he needed me when he welcomed my going. But, who knows, he may be missing me now." She turned back when she had reached St. Cloud and retraced her footsteps easily; in less than an hour she had reached the Pont Royal.

"I have done something that no respectable girl should do," she said as she went up to her room. "I have run the risk of being spoken to in the street. Apparently I am not attractive enough to be in any danger from the vicious," she added as she looked in the glass, but she was pleased with what she saw there and fell asleep at once.

There was a letter from Richard waiting for her asking her to luncheon the following day, and when the time came Anne was overjoyed to see a familiar face once more, though she had been repeating to herself the words she had spoken by the river.

The door of the studio was opened by Ginette, who held out a cool hand. As the girl turned to lead her in, Anne looked at the dark head with the short black hairs cropped close to the brown neck and such envy filled her at the sight that she nearly burst into tears. To be cool and dark and brown, to live in a studio with two men, to talk French, such were the hopeless ambitions which filled her heart. Grandison got up from his chair as she came in but he said nothing, only bowed and sat down again with his eyes on her face. Richard was washing his hands in the corner. "Don't come near me, Anne, I am covered with paint," he called out, but his voice sounded friendly as though he were glad to see her.

Ginette laid her hand on her shoulder: "You are very beautiful," she brought out laboriously. She had been practising the phrase all the morning, and the unexpected words set Anne blushing with pleasure. "Richard has said much of you but not that you are beautiful. He is bad."

Anne's blush was a blush of happiness, and she caught the French girl by the hand and pressed it. Ginette laughed and raised her eyebrows, and would have spoken if they had not been startled by Grandison, who ordered them to sit down to luncheon.

"I have brought some of the drawings I did for fashion-plates to show you," said Anne, but Richard did not refer to them when the meal was over; he seemed more interested in Dry Coulter than in Paris, and began to speak of the village while his companions sat in silence.

"I have heard from Rachel: she is very excited as she is going to be chosen Queen of the May. You know May-day is even more of an institution than Plough Monday," he said, turning towards Grandison.

"It is celebrated more pleasantly in an English village than in Paris." And Richard began to describe how five little girls were chosen, of whom Rachel would be the leader, to go from house to house carrying an arbour of flowers and singing whatever songs they happened to know.

"The arbour is made of cowslips and may, with a few of the early purple orchids," said Anne, calling up the memory of May-day a year ago. "It was raining when they came to the vicarage and they wore yellow ribbons and sang 'Ta ra ra Boom de aye.' I opened the door and they went on singing without paying any attention to the sixpence I held out to them."

"That sixpence went to the chapel Sunday School Treat," said Richard. "Paganism has been made respectable."

"What will Rachel wear as the May Queen?"

"She speaks of a wreath of pansies if there are enough of them out to make it; her companions will have chaplets of forget-me-nots, and they will carry the bower while she carries an armful of tulips. She did not speak of her dress, but of course it will be a white one, and they will wear black worsted stockings and solid little hob-nailed boots laced high up the leg."

"Rachel doesn't worry about her boots," said Anne at once, and her thoughts flew back to Mr. Yockney, then she looked round the studio thinking that the rent was paid out of the grocer's shop at home. " I think Rachel's perfectly happy. I think all your family are," she said.

" So they ought to be," said Richard, laughing. " See what a good son I am. I give my father an object in life, which is more than any of you do. He is very happy and proud of me. In the old days of course," Richard went on, " the first of May was a great affair, with a maypole set up and a Jack of the Green. The May Queen was not a little girl in those days. You would have been chosen instead of Rachel and, having been kissed by all the boys in the village, you would have got rid of your obsession about never getting to know anyone."

Anne blushed uncomfortably, and looked at Grandison who must, she thought, have repeated what she had said while he was seeing her home. " An obsession about never getting to know anyone! " and she wondered if Richard had summed her up for ever in these un-kind words.

"I expect the maze was laid out on a May-day," said Richard, "and the monument is nothing more than a stone maypole, or something with the same signification."

"I can tell you about the monument," said Anne. "It commemorates the restora-tion of Charles II, and was put up by a young man of nineteen, who must have come back from France with the King and recovered his sequestered estate:—a small enough one I should guess, and the Old Hall. I suppose the maze might have been cut on a May-day, and no doubt they had a maypole on the green again: they had been put down under the Commonwealth, but I doubt if there were many to dance. All the better people had served in Cromwell's regiments. Ex-cept in Huntingdon itself, they were all Puritans."

"Then we must imagine your young cavalier setting up a maypole on the green and dancing with gipsy girls and all the riff-raff he could assemble, while the village people held aloof under the elm trees round the edges of the green and prayed for a thunderstorm," said Richard.

"There were oak trees in those days, not elms," said Anne.

"How do you know that?" he asked her sharply.

She knew positively, but she had forgotten how she knew and, as she repeated that she was sure, she felt that she must seem very stupid to Mr. Grandison.

"Well, he danced in a scarlet coat with lace ruffles, which he had brought back from France, with the gipsy girls in their rags, and Maggie Pattle joined in for the sake of the beer, but all the respectable tenants stood under the oak trees looking glum and hating him. But how do you explain that the monument is still standing and, that though it is the most striking thing in the village, nobody ever looks at it or knows anything about it? If one asks a question they just shake their heads and change the conversation."

"The young cavalier lived to be eighty-eight," answered Anne. "It is natural that nobody would dare disturb his maze while he was living, or to pull down the stone column sculptured with his arms. All the Puritans were dead before he was, and the significance of the monument was forgotten by 1729."

" But the civil war isn't forgotten,"
said Richard.

" I have often heard a villager say
when someone has got into trouble for
poaching hares: ' We want another of
the Cromwells in this country. There
were no game laws in Nolly's time.' "

" I expect there is a tradition that the
maze represents something out of harmony
with the village: they have ignored it for
so long that they have forgotten everything except that it is something which
ought to be ignored," said Anne.

Richard agreed with her, and an hour
passed before she remembered the drawings she had brought to show him.

" Leave them for me to look at," said
Richard, but she would not be put off.
As she untied the portfolio she felt that
her fingers were trembling, and she became confused as she explained that she
knew her drawings were not fashionable:
she had done them at Dry Coulter in
ignorance of what the latest fashions
might be, thinking that they would serve
as specimens to show her workmanship.
Instead of explaining this clearly what
she said was something very silly, but
Richard did not smile at her absurdity,

and there was an absolute silence as she laid the first of the drawings on the table, propping it up against a wine bottle.

For a long while Richard Sotheby stood wrinkling his nose and Gerald and Ginette stood silent.

" And the next," said Richard sharply, but, going to the portfolio himself, he turned over the other drawings rapidly. There was a silence again as he carefully fastened the clasp of the portfolio, and then turned and walked a few steps away. Suddenly, however, he began to speak, and the words fell so rapidly that Anne could scarcely follow them.

" Dress designers are very stupid people," he began. " Don't be discouraged when I advise you not to show these actual drawings. In order to create an impression you must first obtain a thorough knowledge of the mode. There is just as much fashion in the drawings of dresses as in the dresses themselves. What would have been all right last year or the year before is quite out of date now." And he began to explain very rapidly what these changes in styles of drawing had been.

He was interrupted suddenly by Ginette.

Anne could not follow her words, but she noticed Grandison nod his head vigorously and say: " An excellent idea," while an expression of exasperation came over Richard's white face.

When he turned to Anne she felt a sudden conviction that her drawings were bad and that Richard was concealing his opinion of them.

" Ginette is of the opinion that you are the right figure, and that you have acquired, Heaven knows how, the right appearance for a mannequin. She wants to introduce you to a man she knows who works in one of the wholesale houses. I think that you would dislike such a life and would soon wish that you were back in England. But don't despair about your drawings," he added, almost shouting the last words.

Anne took up her portfolio, turning Ginette's advice over in her mind.

" How should I get a job as a mannequin? " she asked, but an argument had broken out between Richard and Ginette and her question went for some time unanswered. At last he turned from the French girl in exasperation, and she repeated her question.

" Ginette will let you know," he said. " Come to tea to-morrow at five o'clock." The tone of the invitation was so cross that Anne said good-bye at once. Grandison had scarcely spoken a word during the discussion, but as she left the room he made a gesture as if he would speak, but he said nothing.

" What have I done to upset them all so much? " she asked herself as she hurried down the stairs, but she could find no answer. Richard's words had been encouraging, yet she was tempted to tear up her wretched drawings then and there.

" Yes, my fashion plates are hopeless," she said to herself, but she found it hard to understand why Richard should have been so exasperated by Ginette's suggestion. " If my drawings are no good I must find some other way of earning my living. Richard would keep me in a fool's paradise until my money is exhausted."

Her train of thought was interrupted by the sound of footsteps, and she heard a voice calling her. It was Richard.

" I meant to ask you: if you are short of money, let me lend you ten pounds. You must have time to look about you."

Anne stared at him in surprise. He was

very white; out of breath with running and his words came with an effort, but his tone was still one of exasperation.

"Thank you," she said, looking him in the eyes. "Thank you, I have still seventeen pounds."

"Well, later on," answered Richard. "Whenever you want a loan, come to me. While one has money it is one's duty to share it. That is what Grandison and I believe, and after all you and I come from the same village."

After saying this he turned round and walked back, quietly cursing her existence.

Chapter 14

A REMOVAL

" How could I ever have imagined that I was in love with Richard Sotheby? " Anne asked herself in astonishment as she walked back across Paris. " It turns out I don't love him enough to borrow money from him. He would always behave well, he would always be kind, yet I think he would be delighted if he were never to see me again. I shall never ask him for help or for advice; I shall never go near his studio after to-morrow." And it occurred to her suddenly that the money he had offered to lend her had been earned by his father, and that it might have been spent on Rachel, or on the temperance hotel.

" I wonder why it is that Ginette loves him? " she asked herself. " If she really does. If I were her I should lose my heart to Mr. Grandison." And saying this she recalled the look in Grandison's eyes and how he had kept them fixed on her, how he had seemed to be going to speak and the gesture with which he had sunk back into his chair as she went out of the studio.

"Richard has robbed me of knowing him. We should easily have become intimate, we should have been friends," she said with her heart full of bitterness. Every detail of her walk with Grandison came back and hurt her.

"Well, I am to be mannequin if they like my figure." The more she thought of Ginette's suggestion the better she liked it, and the more difficult she found it to understand Richard's annoyance. She was puzzled to find an explanation, and tried one theory after another, but nothing she could imagine seemed to her probable, and when five o'clock came on the following afternoon she had almost persuaded herself that the explanation of Richard's ill-humour must be something quite unconnected with herself. She knocked and Richard opened the door, and stood for a moment in the threshold before admitting her. He stared at her with a grin on his face and said: "Oh! So it is you, Anne!"

"Weren't you expecting me?" she asked, noticing his surprise. "You said I was to come to tea."

Richard Sotheby led her into the studio, and Ginette rose from the sofa, where she had been lying. The girl's face had changed; Anne could see that she had been crying, but there was so much pride in her greeting that she felt shy of looking her in the face.

" Here is a letter for you," said Ginette gravely, speaking in French and pronouncing her words with the greatest distinctness. " You are to present it personally to M. Kieselyov at that address at eight o'clock to-morrow morning. If he thinks you are in the English style he will engage you."

" Thank you with all my heart. Your goodness . . ." Ginette did not wait for Anne to finish her sentence, but walked away across the room.

Richard was making the tea. " Have you heard from your father? " he asked.

" No, I haven't," said Anne, feeling rather guilty. She had not written to him since her arrival.

" I had a letter from mother with messages for you from Rachel." He was half tempted to add that their names must be coupled together in the village by now, and that this was disagreeable to him, but he looked at Anne and refrained.

She had taken off her hat, and the short, closely cropped hair shone like straw.

There was a worried look on her pale face.

" My God, what innocence! " he said to himself.

" Ginette and Richard have been quarrelling," thought Anne, wondering if Grandison would come in, for she was miserably disappointed not to see him.

But instead of asking if he would be back for tea she said: " I wonder if the swallows are building again in our dove house."

" Do they build there? " asked Richard, and the whole expression of his face altered at her words.

" Yes, they have a nest on the joist. Father leaves the top half of the door open for them and they fly in and out. They are the prettiest of the birds; my favourites, for no birds exceed them in loveliness of colouring: the steel blue back, the crimson throat and the white belly. The flight of the swallow is more beautiful than that of any other bird, but this pair are prettiest when they sit side by side on the rails outside the dove house. Their spirits always seem to me a little low: she moves one wing and then the other, as though she were shrugging her little shoulders, and

then, suddenly, he bursts into song. Do
you know the swallows' song? "

" No," said Richard. " I have never
heard a swallow sing. " He sat down and
buried his face in his hands, and repeated
in tones of utter wretchedness: "No, I
have never heard a swallow sing."

" He has the clear note of a contralto;
not loud or defiant, nor yet feeble but full
of love, subdued because he can never
forget that the world is full of cruelty and
unkindness."

Ginette broke in with a question as to
what Anne had said.

Richard told her, and the French girl
smiled wearily.

" In England it is only the swallows
apparently which have discovered such
platitudes." Then she added: " Why is
she staying? "

" It appears we invited her to tea,"
answered Richard in a low voice.

There was the sound of a heavy tramp
on the stairs and then a knock. Richard
stood up and went to the door. Anne
looked across at Ginette and saw that she
was gazing at her with a strange expression.

" I must go," she said to herself. " Why

does she look at me as if she felt contempt for me?" But it seemed impossible to go after that look without an explanation. The memory of that expression would haunt her.

She looked up and saw that Richard had come back from the door, and that a workman had followed him, and together they crossed the studio and disappeared into the little room at the back.

Anne sat and sipped her tea, tortured by the need to speak, to ask a question, to see light, and by the desire to escape, to go out of the studio and never to set foot in it again. But she could not find the words with which to ask her question or to take her leave, and she sat on, dumbly watching the workman crossing the room, first with a rolled-up mattress in his arms and then with a little folding bed or carrying a wash-hand-stand. Richard came back and threw himself down in a chair. There was a silence, prolonged until the workman reappeared, crossed the studio and went out once more with a chair and a looking-glass.

Ginette gave Richard an appealing look and he said:

" Anne, I think perhaps you had better

go now. Ginette and I are both rather up-set." He paused for a moment and said in colourless tones: " Besides, someone who wishes to see you is waiting."

Anne rose. " Goodbye, Mademoiselle Lariboisière," she said, holding out her hand. The brown hand gripped hers firmly.

" Till we meet again," she said, and then added in broken English: " You have a lucky face."

" Thank you for telling me about the swallows," said Richard as he stood above her at the top of the stairs.

The French workman was struggling with a small table on the staircase and it was some moments before she could reach the street.

"Never to know the meaning! Never to learn the secret! Never to understand anything at all! " Anne cried with tears coming into her eyes. " I have never seen into another person's heart. I never shall. Wherever I am, my curse clings to me! " A vague project of suicide, of being found floating in the river, passed through her mind as she stepped out into the street. The workman was still in front of her lifting the table into a small motor-van; in avoiding him she ran into Grandison's back.

"Good God! You here! Don't go away!" he exclaimed, as though she was running from him. Anne stepped back and stood for a moment staring in astonishment into his red face.

His words sounded angry, and his blue eyes glittered angrily so that she felt afraid and her first impulse was to run back into the house. "I cannot go up there again," flashed through her mind, and she turned again to Grandison.

"Miss Dunnock," said the young man, still looking at her, almost murderously. "I must make an explanation."

The word explanation caught her ears. "No, that is impossible," she said to herself for some reason. "An explanation is impossible."

"I don't understand," she said in a weak voice, giving up all thoughts of flight. She was almost in tears. "I don't understand anything."

Grandison's anger or passion seemed suddenly to have completely disappeared. He looked at her appealingly with an expression in which she could read pity for her and misery on his own account. For a moment he tried to speak and choked, and then, swallowing, went on rapidly:

"It is rather complicated. I am taking away my furniture to a new room and must superintend the man unpacking it. If you could come with me in the van we could talk to each other."

The van was packed; the man was waiting, impatient of their conversation. Anne did not hesitate, but scrambled up onto the tail-board of the van and settled herself on the rolled-up mattress.

She was excited without knowing why, and suddenly, looking at Grandison perched beside her on the edge of the washhand stand, she felt happy and secure.

"I want to explain," he said suddenly, as though he were defending himself. "This is my furniture. I am taking it away from the studio because I cannot live with Richard or with Ginette any longer. I have broken with them completely, and have taken a room of my own."

There was so much suffering in his voice that Anne understood that there had been a quarrel. At that moment all seemed suddenly to have become clear to her, and she felt that she was a very experienced person. "What foolishness!" she exclaimed to herself.

"Why should they have quarrelled?" And she decided to persuade Grandison to turn back.

"Why do you want to leave them?" she asked gently. She was preparing to reason with him sympathetically, and softly to lead him back to Richard. For a moment Grandison sat silent, and something in his sullen expression, his trembling lip and the way in which he opened and then shut his hand, moved her very much.

"I must explain," he repeated. "Ever since I met you at the station I have been madly in love with you."

Anne felt cold all over as she heard these words; she shivered and gazed at Grandison with frightened eyes, asking herself if she had heard what he had said aright; a suspicion crossed her mind that he was playing a joke on her, a heartless, practical joke. She gazed at him in terror, but he went on without turning his head to look at her: "It has been awful. I could not speak to you while I was still living in Richard's studio. I think Ginette guessed but Richard did not suspect until I told him after you went yesterday. I did not think it would upset him so much or that it would upset me so much."

"I don't understand why he should be upset or why he dislikes me, but I feel he does. There has never been anything between Richard and me," said Anne. She stopped, feeling that she had said something foolish.

"I know, but there has been a great deal between Richard and me," answered Grandison. "Just now he hates you, though it is not your fault that I am in love with you, and he knows that."

"He has got Ginette," said Anne.

"Oh, my God!" cried Grandison making the most awful face. "Ginette was my mistress. Surely you knew that?"

Anne gazed at the cuff of Grandison's coat: a check material with a little wavy thread of purple running among the fawns and greys. She was overcome with shame and confusion at her ignorance and her stupidity. There was a long silence.

"This doesn't seem like a trick," she said to herself, but the fear that Grandison might in some way be playing some strange and terrible joke at her expense remained at the back of her mind.

" For some reason I thought that Ginette and you were the same person before I arrived," she said. " You see I overheard Richard spelling out a telegram to you in French before I had ever spoken to him."

" A telegram? " Grandison asked in astonishment. " Oh, yes, perhaps he did telegraph. I wrote and told him that I was in love with Ginette and that I proposed taking her to live with us. . . . That was a dreadful thing to have done. You see, Richard was very fond of me; he cares about nobody else," he said suddenly, wiping the sweat off his forehead.

" I have always, all my life, mismanaged my love affairs. But that is because I have never been in love before. Now I am in love with you and I determined not to mismanage that but to make a clean sweep of everything."

This remark, and the defiant tone in which it was uttered, struck Anne as comic; she laughed but immediately regretted having done so, for Grandison burst into tears.

She had never seen a man weep before and was alarmed. The tears streamed down his cheeks and hung on the stubble of his beard, for he had not shaved that day, and then fell one after another onto his knees.

Anne jumped up from the mattress, hitting her head on the top of the van. " Oh! Damn! " She clutched Grandison round the shoulders while her eyes filled with tears from the pain. " Don't cry; I have hit my head such an awful crack, but you see I am not crying," she said, hugging him and then slipping onto her knees. He looked at her, and the van pulled up with a jerk just as they found each other's faces in a kiss. They alighted, and Grandison led the way into the meanest building that Anne had ever seen. His room was on the top floor, and as they ascended, an odour of cooking, of accumulated filth, of bugs and of boiled rags took them by the throat. But they climbed on, up and up, and behind them toiled the indignant workman, sweating under the mattress in his arms, and pausing to curse the smells and the filthiness of the house under his breath.

" The view is magnificent," said Grandison with a sweep of his arm as he threw open the door of a tiny attic.

" Put the things down anywhere, just

as you like," he added to the workman. He was right, the view was magnificent. All Paris lay glittering at their feet in the sunshine, and Anne forgot the malodorous staircase as she leant out of the open window.

"Yes, the view is lovely," she said, turning to Grandison, but an altercation was going on with the workman, who was repeating again and again: "This place stinks."

Grandison could understand the words well enough, but he was offended and resolutely shrugged his shoulders, repeating: "Don't understand. Fetch my furniture."

"This place stinks," repeated the workman with appropriate gestures. "It gives me a bad throat." He made sounds as if he were going to be sick.

"I don't understand what you say; fetch the furniture, repeated Grandison in a rage, and began to push the man out of the room. "A house full of Poles and bugs," said the man as he made off down the staircase.

"It's quite an accident," said Grandison, "that there is such a wonderful view. I took the first room I could find, by candle

224

light. It is dirty, but I had it scrubbed out with disinfectant this morning. I shall get some sulphur candles in case what he says about the bugs is true."

Anne sniffed: a smell of Jeyes' fluid hung in the air. They were silent, gazing out of the window, waiting while the slow tramp of feet and muttered curses drew nearer and the man came in carrying the bed.

"It stinks," he announced, returning to Richard.

Grandison cursed suddenly with great obscenity in fluent French.

"You mustn't talk to me like that," answered the man, but he left the room after looking at Anne with an air of icy disapproval. "Damn the fellow," said Grandison, and they remained silent while the table, the washhand stand, a piece of drugget and the chairs were brought in.

Grandison had recovered his temper by then, and gave the man a tip. "One doesn't say such things," said the workman, pocketing it, and he went down the stairs clearing his throat. They listened to the tramp of feet descending the stairs without looking at each other, and stood motionless through the minutes of dead silence which followed. "He must be waiting and poking about in the hall," was their unspoken thought and, exchanging a swift glance, they nodded their suspicions. A sudden crash resounded up the stairs of the outer door being slammed, and they smiled happily at each other, for love is impossible except in secret. But although they smiled the silence continued, their hearts beating faster and faster and confusion coming upon them.

"We must put up the bed," said Anne.

Grandison helped her mechanically; the pleasure of her presence near him was so great that he was afraid to speak lest some word of his might scare her away. Together they unfolded the legs of the narrow iron bedstead, set it upon its feet, covered it with a weedy mattress and a coverlet. Then they laid the carpet on the floor, set the trunk in one corner, the washstand in another, and put the table in the middle of the room. There was nothing more to be done, and after speaking once or twice of buying such necessaries as a broom and a looking-glass, they became silent again, Anne sitting in the only chair, Grandison upon the bed, while darkness closed in on them very slowly.

It seemed to the girl then that at last she had found what she had been seeking.

"I have found this room," she said to herself, and already she was at home in it, and she sat musing over the vast landscape of the future, of which she had suddenly caught a glimpse as she had of Paris itself, but without knowledge and unable to recognise the landmarks.

But at last rousing herself, she looked about her and asked suddenly: "How will you paint in such a small room?"

"I don't know," he answered. "I only paint because Richard does."

"It has got dark," she said. "I can't see your face."

He struck a match and they looked at each other.

"I haven't got a candle," he said apologetically. "And there is no gas."

Anne rose from her chair. "She is going," Grandison said to himself as he stood up. Their hands touched and they embraced. "I have always loved you. Before I knew you. Before I knew myself, while I was still in the navy," he whispered rapidly between his kisses.

The whispering went on and on in the dark room, lit by the flickering arc lamps in the street below. Each whisper was a charm that breathed love into her, that stole away her strength, and that changed her nature. Yet Anne still held herself alert, danger seemed near; at any moment a heavy footstep might sound upon the stairs, or a voice break in. It seemed to her that if she sat very still the danger might pass, and when Grandison's voice rose she stroked his hair nervously—hair as short and thick and soft as fur.

"Richard—the danger is Richard," she said to herself, recognising that she was helpless in face of that danger.

Hours passed but no footstep sounded on the stairs, and no voice spoke out of the darkness; only the moon breaking through the clouds flooded the room with light, showing them to each other. They became hungry, but they forgot their hunger, remembered the passage of time and as soon forgot it, grew sleepy and did not think of sleep.

A clock struck and they counted eleven strokes.

"You must be hungry," said Anne.

"Yes, I am," answered Grandison surprised, but he took an apple from his pocket, and when they had shared it their hunger seemed to be satisfied.

A clock struck, and they lost count of the strokes.

"It is midnight," said Anne. "I must go back to my hotel." But she did not move, and an hour later she had consented to stay the night, had undressed in the dark and had got into the bed, while Grandison had wrapped himself in his overcoat and covered with the piece of drugget, was stretched out upon the floor.

For a long while Anne went on stroking his hair, and when at last they fell asleep he was still grasping her hand in both of his and holding it to his lips.

"What's the matter?"

A strangled cry of "Help!" was ringing in her ears, but she understood that it was her own voice that she had heard.

"What's the matter, Anne?"

"It is all right," she answered, coming to herself, but her voice was full of fear, and Grandison, sitting up by her bed, could see her shudder.

"I suppose it was a dream," she murmured, and suddenly the fear left her as the details of her nightmare came back, and she lay in silence piecing them together.

"It was something awful about my father," she said. "I was alone, quite alone, in the vicarage. There was no furniture; I went from room to room looking for my father, but all the rooms were empty; all the furniture had been taken away but they had left me behind. Suddenly I looked out of the bedroom window, my father's bedroom, for it was at the front of the house, and as I expected I saw a Ford van stop at the gate and people getting out of it." Anne shuddered again violently and Grandison began stroking her shoulder. "Don't tell me if it frightens you," he said.

"Two women came first, and I was frightened of them because I could see that they were imbecile from the way they walked, but I was more frightened of the men. They weren't mad but I could see madness in their faces, and I recognised them at once. They were the Puttys, who used to live in the Burnt Farm, but it seemed to me that they were coming to our house. They looked from side to side with wooden faces, and I could see that underneath their woodenness they were full of terror. When they got to the door I could no longer see them, for I dared not look down on their heads, but I heard them unlock the door and knew that they had come to take possession. All I could do was to hide, and for a long while I lay holding my breath and listening as they laughed and screamed and threw plates at each other downstairs. Then I heard the man coming up the stairs in his heavy hobnail boots. I heard him fumble at the door and I began to scream."

"Poor creature," said Grandison. "Who were these people?"

"The Puttys; Richard's mother told me their story: they lived at the Burnt Farm," answered Anne, and stopped, realising that her words could mean nothing to Grandison.

"You aren't frightened any longer, are you?" he asked, and his jaws were pulled apart violently in a yawn; he shivered all over. When he could speak again he repeated: "You are quite sure that you aren't frightened any longer?" He leant towards her to kiss her, but stopped, feeling another yawn upon him.

"No, why should I be?" she replied, and without waiting to hear what else she had to say he lay down on the bare boards and was asleep.

Anne's fear had gone, but one thing still puzzled her; for though she had no memory of her father in her dream she knew that it was terrifying because of him, not because of the Puttys.

" Yes, the subject of my dream was my father," she repeated to herself, wondering suddenly what she was doing in Paris, and hearing a slight snore she looked over the edge of the bed at the sleeping figure beside her.

" Why am I here? " she thought. " This is madness! " and she determined to get out of bed and dress and hurry away if she could do so without waking her neighbour. A minute passed while she waited for him to fall sound asleep, but he stirred uneasily when she sat up in bed. " I must give him five minutes," she thought. " Then I shall be rested." She lay back, aware that a task awaited her which would need all her strength, but before two minutes had passed she began breathing gently and was asleep herself.

Chapter 15

HONEYMOONING

A MONTH had passed, and in the last week of their honeymoon Mr. and Mrs. Grandison were staying at an hotel in Avignon. The sun was already hot when Anne came down to breakfast after waking her husband and leaving him to shave and to dress. The American ladies smiled at her as she came into the little courtyard, bidding her: "Good morning," and hoping that she had passed a pleasant night.

A pleasant night! What could she answer to them? But Anne smiled back, and then she laughed, for she was happy to be alive, and her skin tingled with pleasure as she took her seat carelessly under the flowering oleander. A dog ran in from the street causing a diversion, the cat sunning herself on the cobblestones leapt onto one of the tables; the dog yapped, but he was in no mood for cats, and hearing his master's whistle he ran out again. But watching them Anne felt as much excitement as if she had never seen a cat and a dog before. Her eyes were still bright with interest when the waiter came up with coffee, and he also asked if she had slept well. On the tray there were two letters, one for her and one for Monsieur.

The first letters for three weeks! And Anne seized hers, forwarded from her hotel in Paris, and tore it open. It was from her father and ran as follows:

The Vicarage, Dry Coulter,
Huntingdonshire.

My dear Anne,

The news of your marriage is not such a great surprise as you anticipated, but it is not the less welcome because I had an inkling that what moved you to fly abroad was much the same as that which moves the whitethroat to fly here in summer.

Dear girl, I write strangely removed from you and the blessing I send is a more disinterested one than parents are usually in a position to give. My revelation has come to me late in life, but I am aware that it has changed me greatly, so that now I find it almost impossible to think of worldly things. However, I have packed up the old silver teapot which was your mother's and have had it sent to you addressed

234

to the Paris branch of our bank at
Linton for greater safety. . . . You
shall have the rat-tail spoons, but one
seems to be mislaid. Your letter was
the first communication for many weeks
to recall me to this transient world,
and to that extent I must admit that
your marriage caused me pain. But no,
I am wrong, something else has happened since you left—a sad tragedy.

You will remember our little angelic
visitors of the dove house, so faithful
to one another and so happy as they
chased the summer flies. You will recol-
lect the pleasure he gave us with his
song, always rather saddened, whilst
she brooded over her mysteries in the
little clay cup on the joist. Old Noah
had occasion to go into the upper story
of the dove house and carelessly (for
it was nothing but carelessness) left the
hatch open. I did not notice anything
for several days, then, going up myself, found the swallow dead. She must
have flown up, attracted by the light,
and have beaten her life out on the
window-panes. He, poor fellow, had
flown away. I pray that neither you
nor your husband should ever know

his sorrow. My best regards to the gentleman with the beautiful name, your husband.

Your affectionate Father,
CHARLES DUNNOCK.

P.S. It gives me peculiar pleasure to inscribe Mrs. Grandison on the envelope.

Anne smiled as she finished the letter, but her heart was troubled; never before had her father been so intimate with her —never had he revealed so much of himself. Her love for him came back to her, a sudden shock astonishing her, for it was a love of which she had hardly suspected the existence, while at the same moment she thought: " He can afford to write to me like this now I am safely married and he is in no danger of my coming back."

Soon her emotion passed, and she looked around her with renewed excitement. " How lovely the blue sky and the blossom of the oleander! " The waiter was standing beside her setting out the coffee-pot and the milk jug, the cups and saucers, the two hot rolls, wrapped in napkins, and the four thin bricks of lustreless sugar. She picked up her husband's letter and glanced at the envelope.

"How happy it will make Grandison to have a friendly letter from Richard!" she thought, recognising the handwriting, and she sat wondering if after all the letters they had written to him and the postcards they had sent, he still remained cold and unforgiving.

"He loved Grandison; he cared for nobody else and yet Grandison never gave him any happiness and never showed him any consideration. I cannot bear to think of his feelings after they parted in anger on my account. But this letter must be to say that he has become reconciled to the marriage; he would not write otherwise."

Richard had sent a wedding present, but when they had gone to the studio they found it locked, and after the third or fourth fruitless visit the *concierge* had told them that he had gone away.

Anne looked again at the letter, and saw that it bore an English stamp and that the postmark was Dry Coulter; Richard must have gone home suddenly on a surprise visit.

"It is strange how real Dry Coulter is to me! I was unhappy while I was living there, yet all my memories of it are beautiful, and nowhere else in the world seems so real as that village. Are the English elms more beautiful than the olives? Is the song of the blackbird as lovely as Fleury's flute? Why do I remember every detail of my life before my marriage and nothing of the things that happen to me now? Nothing is real to me now but Grandison, my happiness in him is such that I can enjoy no other beauty."

And Anne reminded herself how she had been with him to the opera and to students' balls in Paris night after night, but the memory of them was already dim, a lovely voice thrilling her for a moment, a sea of lights, a crowd of faces.

"I cannot keep my attention fixed on the stage," she said to herself. "At every moment I have to turn to glance at him, to look at his blunt healthy features, his soft and furry hair, his round head, so like a seal's or an otter's, thrust suddenly above the surface of the water. All I remember of the opera, of the picture galleries, and of the castles which we saw yesterday, is catching Grandison's eye to see whether he were moved by the same things that moved me—and because of that I felt no emotion except about him."

She laughed, but her happiness was coloured with the regret that her only opportunity of seeing so many beautiful things should have been during her honeymoon.

"We should have been just as happy if we had stayed in that horrid room with the beautiful view." And Anne recalled how they had spent their first days held in a web of unrealities, making declarations, mumbling affadavits before a consul, handing telegrams through wire netting, and patiently waiting for permission to get married. "Days vague and as impossible to remember as the waving of weeds seen through water," she said. But Sir John, who had cut off his son's allowance while he was living in Paris with Richard Sotheby, had been pleased at the marriage and had sent a cable with his blessing and a thousand pounds from Ceylon. . . . And dismissing the past, Anne paused for a moment to wonder what their life would be like in future. Grandison had consented to live in London and to take the job his father had offered him in the tea business.

"How long he is, dressing!" she exclaimed, and jumping up she ran up the yellow stairs to their bedroom.

She had forgotten to take Richard's letter with her, but it was the first thing she spoke of.

" You've been using my powder puff," she added, for his shaven cheek was delicious with scent.

" Stingy! Stingy! If there is anything I hate it's stinginess! " he exclaimed, embracing her again. She fought with him but was overcome; they laughed, but their laughter changed suddenly to the seriousness of love-making.

" What a devil you are, Anne, slipping out of bed like a mouse without waking me until the moment you were going down to breakfast."

" It is difficult to wake you," she answered. " And I always feel a criminal when I do."

" You are a sly hypocrite. But I vowed I would not come downstairs this morning until you had come up again to find me. You see your tricks don't work."

" For all you know I might have gone out with the American ladies."

" I should have stayed here all day."

" We are scandal enough as it is in this hotel," she answered.

" Just as we were at Dijon."

" If you will go down alone to break-fast, naturally you cause a scandal. People think something dreadful must have happened. They see that you care nothing for me, Anne. Love means nothing to you."

Her looks were a sufficient answer to his reproaches, and he was silent as she seized him and bent over him.

" Keep still," she whispered. Looking up, Grandison could see the ceiling of the darkened room striped with bars of light from the upturned slats of the shutters. Outside, the sunlight poured into the grilling street; an electric tram passed by, its passage announced by the swishing of overhead wires and followed by the crackling of electric sparks. Wrapped in the weakness of love, Anne and Grandison lay at each other's mercy; each tiny movement was agony to them.

" Keep still! Keep still! " A cry broke from their lips, and then, in the solitude of perfect unity, they fell asleep. The overhead wires swished, an electric tram lurched past the hotel on grinding wheels, above which the soft crackle of electricity came like the sound of a silk skirt. Already the American ladies had left the hotel, the waiter in the courtyard had cleared away the cold coffee and the uneaten rolls; the forgotten letter had been handed in at the manager's office; the chambermaid had looked through the keyhole and had gone away to wash vegetables in the kitchen, before either husband or wife spoke.

" What time is the bus? " he asked, girding his silk trowsers with a sash.

" In five minutes! " screamed Anne, looking at the gold wrist watch that Richard Sotheby had given her. Grandison seized his pocket-book and cigarettes, they snatched up their Panama hats and fled down the cool staircase with its smell of varnish and of glue, out into the baking heat of the street.

There was no taxi to be seen and no tram.

" Run! " he cried, and they ran, though the air came hot to the mouth and the sun slashed through their silk shirts, scorching their shoulders. They were late, but the char-a-banc had waited for them, and when Grandison had cried out: " No breakfast! " it waited while he rushed into the station buffet and came back with a bottle of sweet champagne, a long roll of bread and a green water-melon. They sat in the front seats, and the oil cloth cushions ran with their clean sweat, while they were drinking champagne out of the palms of their hands and spilling it over their knees as the heavy car lurched and bumped on the road. They laughed, and the melon juice ran over their chins, and into their ears; they spoke their thoughts aloud heedless of the American ladies and the party of English school-teachers behind them, and the whole char-a-banc of twenty people was united by the happiness of watching them. Looking at the outlines of their shoulders, everyone was moved to a gay, slightly tipsy sentimentality; the discomfort of a whole day's jolting, of being a school-teacher and wearing stays, or a double-breasted waistcoat and starched collars and side-whiskers, all such ills passed unnoticed. As for the lovers, they paid no attention to their companions and scarcely even looked at the sights they had come to see. Strolling through the Roman theatre and the bull-ring at Arles, they made silly jokes about asparagus, and on the way home broke into their first quarrel, Anne maintaining that a cigale was a grasshopper, while Grandison reiterated that it was a sedentary dragonfly with a beetle's body.

" A letter for you, Sir," said the porter as they entered the hotel, and they looked at each other in embarrassment, wondering how they could have come to have forgotten Richard's letter. A word from him meant so much to both of them! But recollecting how it was that they had so nearly missed the bus that morning, they broke out laughing.

" Bad news," said Grandison, his face changing suddenly. " Richard's father, the grocer, has gone bankrupt. The worst is that I cannot help feeling I have had my share in causing it by my cursed extravagance. Richard paid for everything for me, and for Ginette." As he said this his face flushed scarlet.

"It is more likely to be the hotel," said Anne.

" Yes, that is what Richard says, and then there is a message about your father," he added, handing her the letter. His face was still flushed, but the first feeling of shame had passed into one of anger with the outside world that threatened to break in upon his happiness.

Dry Coulter.

Dear Seal,

Why do you and Anne send me so many postcards? I ask because I got six yesterday; very disturbing when I am doing my best to forget you. " Let the dead bury their dead." What does that mean? Perhaps I have got the phrase wrong, but for some reason though I don't understand what it means I find it expresses my feelings.

So don't send me any more postcards. I shall think of you and Anne quite as much as you deserve, and I shall want to see you directly you come back to England.

You ask me also what I think of your compact with your father, and your giving up painting. I have no opinion about it: you must settle your own affairs as you think best. If you mean: do I think you would have been a good painter if you went on, I don't. But I think you might have eventually done something else, I mean something serious, and badly as I think of you I still believe you capable of something better than being a tea-merchant in Mincing Lane. That seems to me a frivolous waste of time. One only has one life.

I have plenty to distract me here: my father has involved himself in a tiresome disaster. He has gone bankrupt with no assets but an unfinished hotel with water-logged foundations, which would have flooded every winter. He has taken to his bed with a bad heart attack, and I have spent a hectic fortnight finding out the exact position. Meanwhile I have arranged for a show in Bond Street, and have got a commission to paint a portrait. I am setting up in London. The only drawback is that England always gives me indigestion. My mother is quite unmoved by the bankruptcy.

Please tell Anne that I haven't seen her father, but from what I can hear his position is much more serious. He has given up taking the services in church, and people think that he is definitely odd. The vicarage certainly looks odd; he wouldn't open the door to me. I think Anne ought to come down as soon as possible. I will do what I can but I have got my hands full just now.

Rachel sends her love; she is a pretty creature. I shall have to begin to think about sending her to Newnham in a year or two. There: I know you can't help your character (a bad one) any more than I can help mine, so don't let's think of our characters and don't send me any more postcards or letters.

Au Revoir,

RICHARD.

P.S. Ginette has got the job she meant for Anne, as a mannequin *style anglais*. She writes to me *every day*. Whose fault is that?

Anne crumpled the letter in her hand; she did not feel shame or anger as her husband had done; she had no irritation against the outside world but only pity. As she followed her husband to the stairs her mind was busy with plans for returning to England. She thought of her father, of the old grocer lying in bed, staring at the ceiling, and of Mrs. Sotheby.

" All the same, we were right to send Richard all those postcards; he would have been more unhappy without any news of us." Grandison was stamping about the room in a rage.

" It means no more to me than a famine in China," he said.

" We had better pack our things; we shall have to go home to-morrow," answered Anne.

In the train the outside world became once more " like the waving of weeds seen through water," a series of noises, smells, and movements which concerned them little, and they did not speak of the future until they were on the boat, when Anne said: "Let's deal with our affairs separately: while you are arranging with your father's firm I will go down to Dry Coulter."

Grandison nodded, and realising that the cliffs before him were indeed those of Dover, that an interview with his uncle and his elder brother awaited him, and that his father would be back in England in a few days, a bitter regret seized him that he had ever seen Anne.

" Love for this woman is ruining my life," he said to himself, but when he turned his head and he found himself gazing into her pale, fierce, happy face, he understood that he was helpless. He looked at his wife's short straw-coloured hair, her intense grey eyes and her slim body, and listening to her abrupt speech he told himself that everything else was unimportant.

"I am glad I didn't buy a bicycle," said Anne. She had been thinking for a moment of the past.

Chapter 16

ANGELS

THE train reached Linton station at last, and Anne leaped out of the stuffy carriage, all the weariness of her long wait at Cambridge forgotten in the excitement of seeing again what she had so often seen before. She could not hide the eagerness in her voice as she handed her bag to the porter, asking him to give it to the carrier.

" Well, Miss, are you glad to be back?" he asked, recognising her.

" Yes, of course I am," she answered, and smiling with surprise she made her way across the market-place.

Linton was unchanged, and she was filled with joy and gratitude to the little town, believing that it could never alter in the future and not reflecting that it was scarcely three months since she had set off with even greater excitement on her way to France in the belief that she would never see Linton again.

She walked on, and turned down Bridge Street, rejoicing to see the signs over the shops and the faces of the shopmen who were standing in their doorways looking out for the last customers before closing—all familiar things and persons. On the crest of the bridge she paused and looked back, thinking that on the morrow she would have met Grandison at the station and would be walking with him through the streets of the old town. A lorry coming towards her filled the bridge, and she took shelter in one of the angles of the parapet. Looking down over the side, she watched the waters of the Ouse slipping away from the masonry of the piers, and hoped that she would see a fish, but no fish showed itself, and when she lifted her eyes she was startled by the sight of an addition to the landscape, the beginnings, surely, of Mr. Sotheby's hotel. There was a huge hole excavated by the edge of the river, filled with muddy water, a mound of blue clay, an ordered pile of white glazed bricks, a few wheelbarrows upside down, a lot of drain-pipes and nothing else.

" So perish all innovations! " Anne exclaimed, and recollecting how the old grocer had talked to her three months before, and seeing his tragedy before her, she began to laugh.

" I wonder if Richard laughed when he

251

saw that hole full of water? Yes, to be sure he did, for we all laugh at our parents, we understand them so well," but her thoughts turning suddenly to her own father, she sighed in despair and walked on.

She had scarcely left the bridge when she caught sight of the grocer himself. He was sitting bolt upright, driving his flea-bitten white pony, his head thrown back, and his white beard sticking out in front of him. "Like a billy-goat looking up to Heaven," thought Anne. "Yet he is like Richard too, he has the same foxey nose."

"Good evening, Mr. Sotheby," she called out. The pony had dropped to a walk as she spoke, but the old man's eye fell stonily on her and he made no answer to her greeting. When he had passed, Anne looked after him in doubt whether she had been deliberately ignored or had not been recognised, or perhaps not even heard, and she saw that the old dog-cart had been lately repainted and newly varnished; on the back was written in scarlet letters:

"INTERNATIONAL TEA TRUST."

"He looks ill," she thought. "And his illness is that his pride has been wounded. He has been so virtuous and so successful all his life, it is too bad that Grandison and Ginette, and excavating a hole in a river bank should have combined to ruin him." She smiled as she said this, but her thought was broken suddenly by the reflection that her own father was waiting for her and that in less than an hour they would be speaking together. Trouble would be sure to arise between them at once, and each of them would behave with falsity. And reluctant to come to her journey's end, unconsciously she dropped into a slower walk.

The road was long and dusty, and she was glad to turn aside into the footpath by the cross-roads, a footpath that was little frequented, for it was half a mile longer than the road. The first field was so huge that it seemed she would never cross it; there was not a tree on which she could rest her eyes and nothing in it except the tussocky grass underfoot and a dozen thirsty bullocks clustering round an empty cistern by the gate, waiting for the water-cart. A field of ripening wheat lay next, and she pushed her way down the narrow lane between the ears, unable to resist snatching at some of them. The grains were still full of milk, yet there was something dry even in their juiciness which made her clear her throat and wish for a cup of tea. Already she could see the elms of Dry Coulter, and she pushed on, getting at last into the next field where there were men at work with teams of horses harrowing and rolling the dusty earth.

"It is likely enough that these are the men and the horses that came to our door-step in the snow," she said, and soon she had crossed to the far side, where a line of men, bent up double, were strung out across the field. But so big was the expanse that rollers and harrows, men and teams of horses and this string of men dibbling, were so far away that she could not see their faces, and felt as though she were alone.

"They are planting cabbages," she guessed. "Each man leans forward to make a hole with the dibber in his right hand, sticks in a young plant and treads it firm with his left heel as he passes in his stride forward to strike the next hole. So they work all day, and this will be a vast expanse of cabbages before the winter. The life of these men is to labour all day in the sun, or in the rain, in these immense fields, alone for hour after hour, with nothing to speak with but a horse, and to go back at night to sleep in a tiny room with a candle burning in the closed window, then to rise again with the first colour of the dawn. That is the life that the greater number have always led, yet it has hardly touched our thoughts and we live on their labour, drinking the milk and swallowing the buttered toast, thinking of anything rather than of how the cows are kept fat and the thistles and docks are spudded out to make room for the wheat, for there is nothing in all that labour, or in all those lives, to interest us. The labourers themselves are silent about it; there are few songs which take mangels or potatoes as their subject, and when we look for poetry in the fields we turn south to Italy or Greece and the goats nibbling at the vines."

The footpath had been ploughed up, its last traces had disappeared beneath the harrow and the roller, and she walked carefully among the young cabbage plants, withering and grey after the long day's sun. They looked dead, but they would live.

" They would die in a garden unless they were shaded under flower-pots, but everything lives in the fields; perhaps the air is purer under the open sky," thought Anne.

As she crossed into the next field a bird flew out of a poplar tree by the stream. " A hawk," was her first thought, but it surprised her by calling " Cuckoo " as it flew.

" He ought to have changed his tune a month ago. ' In July he gets ready to fly; in August, go he must.' Go he must, go he must," she repeated, and the sentence in her father's letter came back into her mind in which he had compared her to a whitethroat.

" Indeed he was right, for I was under the same compulsion to go as the birds, but my going was harder. At least I fancy so, though the young swallows find it a difficult business to leave England, staying a week or two after the old birds have gone." And Anne was surprised at herself for thinking of the birds with pleasure: in the past she had found her father's love for them so irritating.

" I remember that I wished for a bird for my hat, yet in Paris where I could have worn it, the suggestion would have disgusted me. There, where I was going to the opera, I was always thinking of the birds, and the one beautiful thing that I shall never forget is the shout of the birds' song with which one is woken on a March morning. And how they sing after the rain." She laughed at the contradiction in herself which had made her love in Paris what had so much bored her in England.

"Yet within an hour of my meeting with my father I shall be wishing the cats good hunting," she added smiling.

"How will he greet me I wonder?" —a question which had been repeated so often that it made her ill with apprehension.

"What are the troubles that await me?" She was already at Dry Coulter; the elms rose up before her, and when she had crossed the last field the path would lead her through the churchyard and onto the green. The last field had been cut and the last of the hay was being carried, a little boy drove a clicking horse-rake across her path, and pulling a lever, dropped a thin roll of the last gleanings of hay at her feet; further on two women were raking up the wisps of hay into heaps and a boy was pitching it into a red tumbril where another boy gathered it into his arms and trod it under foot, after which the old mare was led on to the next heap.

Anne could see that the hard work was done, that they were enjoying themselves playing at hay-making, clearing up what the men had left behind. Soon she was out of the hay-field, slipping over the wall of the churchyard, a wall which had been worn smooth by the breeches of generations of labourers, for a short cut to the footpath ran among the graves beneath the limbs of the giant sycamore. She had never liked the tree, sharing her father's jealousy for the little church so far overtopped by it and so overshadowed in summer. If it had not been part of the rookery he would have had it cut down. The nests were hidden now in the leaves, and as she looked up into the tree an old fancy came back into her mind and she said: " The sycamore is like Ely Cathedral, so cool and so airy; to hop from one branch to another must be like sitting first on one chair and then on another; the pigeons shorten wing and alight to rest awhile before they continue their voyages, just as the tourists come in and sit for a few moments before they motor on to Cambridge or King's Lynn."

As she passed the porch she stopped with a new curiosity to read the notices, in the past she had so often written them herself, but the notice which caught her eye brought back all her apprehensions:

NOTICE

Owing to the continued indisposition of the vicar, arrangements have been made for morning service to be held every Sunday by the Reverend J. Grasstalk and the Reverend the Honourable F. H. G. L. à Court Delariver, alternately, until further notice.

F. LAMBERT } *Churchwardens.*
H. BOTTLE }

" That means that father will lose his living unless I can persuade him. . . . I shall have to write to the Bishop. Perhaps if he took a holiday. . . ." Anne hurried on and her spirits rose, for the worst had not happened. She had feared that she would find an inhibition. She opened the lychgate and went out onto the green, passing beneath the elms. There was the little stream, and there lay the old monument and the maze, but her thoughts of her father were dispersed by catching sight of a jumble of yellow derricks, of caravans and steam engines on the green.

"Dry Coulter feast!" she exclaimed in astonishment. "Why it must begin to-morrow! Here are the swing-boats and the roundabouts; here are the show-men and the gipsies." She hurried forward, excited and yet annoyed that her home-coming had chanced to be on the eve of so momentous an occasion as the village feast. "Timed to fall between the hay-making and the harvest," she said to herself. "Richard would tell me that the feast is as much a pagan custom as Plough Monday or May-day. Each of the villages about here has its feast, and they come one after another in the height of summer. They are feasts at which there is little feasting, only a roundabout and swing-boats on the green, but to-morrow the village girls will dance and the men roll up their shirtsleeves and try their strength and run in hurdle races, or win coco-nuts or a cup and saucer."

Under the elms and the beeches the canvas booths were already standing, five or six men were working hard to put up the swings, women were carrying pails of water and the horses, still in their harness, were roaming over the green and cropping the grass. All the travelling people and even their children were working hard; they shouted to each other as they ran to and fro without sparing a glance for the groups of village children, the boys following them and getting in their way, the girls standing and gazing, or sitting close by in the grass. Among one of the groups, sitting and lying on the grass, Anne recognised a friend as she drew nearer.

"Rachel," she called, and the little girl looked up at once, but she hesitated for a moment before rising to her feet and, though she came to meet her, Anne noticed that she walked slowly where a few months before she would have run. The child's shyness caused a like shyness in Anne herself, and they stood facing each other without kissing or shaking hands.

"Thank you very much for the postcards you sent me, Mrs. Grandison," said Rachel. "Richard gave me all the postcards you and Mr. Grandison sent him and I have put them all in my album."

"I wish you could have seen some of

the places we went to, Rachel. A great river, the Rhone, rushes down between the vineyards, and there are castles and wonderful old towns," said Anne, and for a little while she chattered of what she had seen abroad, but ended by saying: " I see they are getting ready for the feast. We went to a wonderful circus at Avignon. I thought of you, Rachel, when I saw it. Grandison won a live pigeon as a prize, for which we had no home so we let it fly from the bridge over the river. It beat its wings and flew crazily this way and that, but at last it lifted itself and disappeared over the battlements into the town. Have you been to any circuses since we went to Linton Fair together? "

There was a look of defiance in the child's face and a hard note in her shrill voice. Her face was paler than ever, but dark under the eyes.

" No, I haven't been to a circus there, Mrs. Grandison. Richard wanted to take me to the feast at Wet Coulter but I wouldn't go."

" You'll enjoy the feast here to-morrow, won't you? "

" Yes, I shall enjoy the Dry Coulter feast, Mrs. Grandison," answered Rachel.

"Come part of the way home with me," said Anne.

"I'll come to the edge of the green."

They walked for a little while in silence.

"You have had your hair cut, Rachel. Was that Richard's doing?"

The little girl blushed scarlet, she hung her head and seemed on the point of bursting into tears. Anne cursed herself for her unfortunate question. "The child must have got creatures in her head; I should have remembered the village better," but she was mistaken in her thought, for when Rachel spoke it was to say: "I heard that you had your hair cut off, Mrs. Grandison."

Anne took off her hat. "Yes," she said, "It is shorter than yours. Did Richard tell you that?" Their eyes met; Rachel had recovered herself. "I am going to let it grow again," she said defiantly. "Father doesn't like it short." She stopped to kick a stone viciously out of her path.

On hearing Mr. Sotheby spoken of, Anne felt strangely embarrassed, and to turn the conversation she asked: "How is your mother? Will you tell her that I am back and that I shall come round to the shop to see her as soon as I can?"

"Mother is not in the shop now," replied Rachel almost rudely.

They had reached the edge of the green, and the little girl stopped short, motionless and stubborn by the little bridge.

"Mother is never in the shop now, nor am I. Father is made the manager, and there is a man under him learning to take his place."

"Is Richard here or in London?" Anne asked. "My husband spent a day looking for him but couldn't find him."

"Richard's busy." This time the rudeness in the child's voice was unmistakeable, and there was a pause whilst Anne looked down into the pale face working with passion. The little girl was trying hard to keep back her tears.

"I'm to go to school at Cambridge. Richard says I am to get a scholarship to go to college."

"Come a little further and tell me about it," said Anne.

Rachel's emotion upset her, and she was tired of standing still.

"No, I must go back now." The little girl was still uneasy, and shifted from foot to foot.

"Well, I daresay we shall meet to-morrow," said Anne, disappointed. She was reluctant to let Rachel go, wanting to find an excuse for delaying her own arrival at the vicarage.

"Let's go to the feast to-morrow and ride on the roundabout together," she said.

Rachel lifted a pale face and gazed at her angrily; two tears ran unheeded down her cheeks and she answered with indignation.

"No, you won't be stopping here long"; then, without waiting for an answer or to say goodbye, she ran back onto the village green. When she had gone a little way she dropped into a walk and soon stopped. She was not in the mood to rejoin her companions; watching the gipsies would no longer interest her, and as soon as Anne had turned the corner Rachel slowly followed in her footsteps.

The rays of the sun were horizontal, and the last strip of turf by the Broad Ditch was striped with the shadows of the elms, the darkest and the most brilliant greens; on the water a crowd of ducklings were swimming eagerly in all directions, in and out of the sunlight; in another half-hour the dew would begin to fall and the little owls would come out to hoot at the cats. Anne turned to look back. Behind her the lower branches of the elms were already in shadow, their tops shone in the sunlight; between the trunks she could see a glimpse of the village green beyond, with the yellow painted roof of a roundabout. There was a silence and suddenly Anne gave a long sigh, a sigh of happiness.

"I am happy now and completely at peace. I was never happy here before, but I am now for I am free. The opinion of neighbours cannot weigh on me, for my life is full and happy and satisfied. Each day is rich and full, and though summer passes it returns again. There are better years coming than any of the years which are passed, and the leaves will always drop in November and spring afresh in May."

The figure of Rachel came into view, and Anne saw the child stop.

"Well, now I must see my father," she said to herself, shrugging her shoulders, a trick she had caught from Grandison; then she turned towards the vicarage, and swinging her arms and shaking her bare head, she walked forward. From a

266

distance the vicarage was black against the sunset, but as she came abreast of it, she saw it clearly, the old familiar building, strangely like a Noah's ark, with a chimney at each end. But the moment that she glanced at it Anne stopped short. The vicarage—it had been burnt! It was a ruin. But the hollyhocks were standing in full flower ; the roses on the wall were not scorched—and Anne could see that there had been no fire: all that had happened was that the windows had been taken out: there was no glass; there were no window-sashes.

Wire-netting had been nailed across each of the down-stair windows, but the bedroom windows were open spaces. Otherwise there was little change; the front lawn had been mowed recently, the path had been weeded, and round the windowless house all the rose-trees were in bloom.

Anne walked slowly up the pathway, noticing everything and reassured by a hundred little details. The box-trees had been clipped. On the doorstep she paused, uncertain whether to try the door-handle or to ring the bell.

" I will ring the bell," she said to herself, lifting her eyes to see if she were being spied upon from upstairs. Through the open windows first one bird flew and then another, a third chased it; then, as the bell jangled in the hall, a whole covey of sparrows flew out over her head.

" The windows have been taken out so that the birds may fly in." The change seemed to her a sensible one for her father to have made. She could hear the shuffling of footsteps inside, and at that moment the thought flashed through her mind that if her father's eccentricities were become such that he could no longer be a clergyman, he would make an admirable bird-watcher on some island sanctuary.

" He would live alone in a hut without seeing anyone for six months of the year, and he would be perfectly happy." Her project filled her with excitement; she longed to talk of it, to find out if she could put it into execution.

The door was flung open and her father stood before her, glaring up at her, for the floor of the house was sunk below the level of the garden, but he showed no sign of recognition. His cheeks were hollow, his tangled beard full of grey hairs and his black, clerical coat was filthy with the droppings of birds; the shoulders and sleeves seeming as if they had been spattered over with whitewash. An unpleasant dirty smell came through the door; in spite of ventilation the house smelled like an old hen-coop.

Anne waited for her father to speak, watching him silently while the anger died out of his gaze. He coughed once or twice, blinked his eyes as if very tired, and said at last in a mild voice: " Well, Anne, my dear."

" Did you get my letter? I have come to pay you a visit, father."

A mischievous, slightly guilty expression came over Mr. Dunnock's face and he coughed again. " I am afraid I didn't read it," he answered. " I hardly know if I can invite you in. You see I am living with the angels now."

There was a long silence. " It was very sweet of you to write such a kind letter about my marriage," said Anne at last. " And to send me Mamma's teapot, and to tell me about the tragedy in the dove house."

" The swallows have come back," said Mr. Dunnock. He spoke eagerly, and stepping out of the house, he took his daughter by the arm and led her round the end of the vicarage. A steel-blue bird circled over their heads and swooped into the open door of the dove house.

" Angels," said Mr. Dunnock, putting a finger to his lips. " They are angels."

THE END

The Westminster Press
411a Harrow Road
London W. 9